She smelled like sugar and frosting and all the things he'd ever longed for. An ache gripped him so hard he had to drag in a breath.

She swayed toward him, those green eyes lowering to his lips. The pulse at the base of her throat fluttered faster and faster. Her hand tightened in his.

He gripped her chin, lifted it, needing to taste her so badly he thought he might fall to his knees from the force of it. Desire licked fire through his veins. His lips started to descend. He moved in close, so close he could taste her breath, but the expression in her eyes froze him.

They glittered. With tears.

"Don't you *dare* kiss me out of pity."

She didn't move out of his hold, and he knew then that she was as caught up in the same grip of desire as him.

"Please, Rick. Don't kiss me because you feel sorry for me."

The tears trembled, but they didn't fall. Every muscle he had screamed a protest, but he released her and stepped back.

He swallowed twice before he was sure his voice would work. "Pity was the last thing on my mind."

The Wild Ones

What will it take to tame these rebels?

A brand-new duet

by Michelle Douglas

Best friends Tash and Rick are in for the wildest of rides when they're forced to spend time on the other side of the tracks.

Reforming a rebel image is tough—especially when the past is against them. But when their future depends on learning to trust someone else, they soon find out that with the right person on their side, they can do anything...even risk it all for love!

Read both books in this amazing duet:

THE REBEL AND THE HEIRESS

August 2014

and

HER IRRESISTIBLE PROTECTOR

July 2014

The Rebel and the Heiress

Michelle Douglas

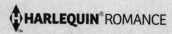
HARLEQUIN® ROMANCE

Recycling programs
for this product may
not exist in your area.

ISBN-13: 978-0-373-74300-1

THE REBEL AND THE HEIRESS

First North American Publication 2014

Printed in U.S.A.

At the age of eight, **Michelle Douglas** was asked what she wanted to be when she grew up. She answered, "A writer." Years later she read an article about romance writing and thought, *Ooh, that'll be fun.* She was right. When she's not writing she can usually be found with her nose buried in a book. She is currently enrolled in an English master's program for the sole purpose of indulging her reading and writing habits further. She lives in a leafy suburb of Newcastle, on Australia's east coast, with her own romantic hero—husband Greg, who is the inspiration behind all her happy endings.

Michelle would love you to visit her at her website, www.michelle-douglas.com.

Recent books by Michelle Douglas:

HER IRRESISTIBLE PROTECTOR**
ROAD TRIP WITH THE ELIGIBLE BACHELOR
THE REDEMPTION OF RICO D'ANGELO
THE CATTLEMAN'S READY-MADE FAMILY*
FIRST COMES BABY...
THE NANNY WHO SAVED CHRISTMAS
BELLA'S IMPOSSIBLE BOSS
THE MAN WHO SAW HER BEAUTY

*Part of the Bellaroo Creek! trilogy
**The Wild Ones

This and other titles by Michelle Douglas are available in ebook format from www.Harlequin.com.

For my little brother, Kyle,
who's always been a rebel in his own way.

CHAPTER ONE

RICK BRADFORD STARED at the Victorian mansion elegantly arranged in front of him and then down at the note in his hand before crumpling the piece of paper and shoving it in his jeans pocket.

He'd checked with his friend Tash earlier. 'You're sure you got that right? Nell Smythe-Whittaker rang and asked if I'd drop round?'

'For the tenth time, Rick, yes! It was the Princess all right. And no, she didn't mention what it was about. And no, I didn't ask her.'

For the last fortnight Tash's brain had been addled by love. His lip curled. Not that he had anything against Mitch King and it was great to see Tash happy but, as far as he could tell, her street smarts had all but floated out of the window. Why hadn't she asked the Princess what this was about?

Because she was viewing the world through rose-coloured glasses, that was why. His lip curled a little more. He wasn't sure he could stand being a third wheel in her and Mitch's hazy, happy little world for much longer. It was time to move on. Tomorrow he'd head up the coast, find work somewhere and…

And what?

He lifted a shoulder.

First he'd find out what Nell Smythe-Whittaker wanted. *You won't find that out by standing here on the footpath like some dumb schmuck.*

Blowing out a breath, he settled a mantle of casual, almost insolent assurance about himself. The people from Nell's world—probably including Nell herself—looked down on the likes of him and he had no intention of giving them, or her, the satisfaction of thinking he cared two hoots either way.

Would Nell look down that pretty autocratic nose at him? He hadn't spoken to her since they were ten years old. He could count the number of times he'd seen her since then—and only ever in the distance—on one hand. They'd never spoken, but she'd always lifted a hand in acknowledgement. And he'd always waved back.

It had never felt real. It had always felt somehow apart from the daily humdrum. He scratched a hand across his face. *Stupid! Fairy tales!* He was too old for such nonsense.

You're only twenty-five.

Yeah? Well, most days he felt as if he was fifty.

Clenching his jaw, he pushed open the gate and strode up the walk to the wide veranda with its ochre and cream tessellated tiles. With an effort of will, he slowed his strides to a saunter and planted a devil-may-care smirk on his face.

Up closer, he could see that Nell's fancy castle needed some attention. Paint peeled at the window trims and flaked here and there from the walls. One section of guttering leaned at a drunken angle and the wider garden was overgrown and unkempt. Here and there he caught sight of the silver wrappers of crisp packets and chocolate bar wrappers winking in the sunlight.

So…the rumours were true then. The Princess had fallen on hard times.

Ignoring a doorbell he had little faith would work, he lifted his hand to knock on the ornately moulded front door when voices from the partially open French windows further along the veranda halted him. Words didn't just drift out on the summer air. They sped.

'You won't get another opportunity like this, Nell!'

A male voice. An angry male voice. Rick's every muscle bunched in readiness. He hated bullies. And he really hated men who bullied women. He stalked down to the windows.

'You are a sleazy, slimy excuse for a man, Mr Withers.'

He paused. Her voice held no fear, only scorn. She could obviously deal with the situation on her own.

'You know it's the only answer to the current straits you find yourself in.'

'Is that so? And I suppose it's a coincidence that this particular solution is one that will also line your pockets?'

'There isn't a bank manager in Sydney who'll loan you the money you need. They're not going to touch that business plan of yours with a bargepole.'

'As you don't happen to be a bank manager and I no longer have any faith in your professionalism you'll have to excuse my scepticism.'

Rick grinned. *Go, Princess!*

'Your father won't be pleased.'

'That is true. It's also none of your concern.'

'You're wasting your not inconsiderable talents.' There was a silence. 'You're a very beautiful woman. We'd make a good team, you and I, Nellie.'

Nellie?

'Stay where you are, Mr Withers. I do not want you to kiss me.'

Rick straightened, instantly alert.

In the next moment a loud slap rang in the air, followed by scuffling. Rick leapt for the window, but it burst open before he could reach it and he found himself pressed back against the wall of the house as Nell frogmarched a man in a shiny suit along the length of the veranda, his earlobe twisted between her thumb and forefinger, and all but threw him towards the gate. 'Good day, Mr Withers.'

The suit straightened and threw his shoulders back. Rick went to stand behind Nell, legs planted and mouth grim. He folded his arms and flexed his biceps.

The suit gave the kind of smirk Rick would give a lot to wipe off his face…except he wasn't that kind of guy any more.

'I see you've your bit of rough. So that's the way you like it?'

'I'm afraid, Mr Withers, you're never going to find out how I like it.' She glanced behind her and met Rick's gaze, her green eyes…beautiful. 'Hello, Mr Bradford.'

Her voice reached out and wrapped around him like a caress. 'Hello, Princess.' He hadn't meant to call her that; it just slipped out. Those eyes widened and continued to stare into his until the breath jammed in his throat.

'Well, you needn't think your bit of rough is going to get you out of your current jam and—'

'Oh, do be quiet, you horrible little man.'

Those green eyes snapped away and Rick found he could breathe again.

And then he looked at her fully and what he saw made him blink. Nell looked as if she'd just stepped out of some nineteen-fifties movie. She wore a dress that made every male impulse he had sit up and stare. It had a fitted bodice that was snug to the waist and a skirt that flared out to mid-calf. It sported a Hawaiian beach print complete with surf, sand and palm trees.

'Mr Bradford is ten times the man you are and what's more he has manners, like a true gentleman.'

He did? In the next instant he shook his head. They were reading from different scripts here.

Without another word, Nell turned and took his arm. 'I'm so glad you could drop around.' And she led him back along the veranda, effectively dismissing the other man. 'I'm terribly sorry. I'd take you through the front door—I don't want you thinking I'm taking you in via the tradesman's entrance or some such nonsense—but I can't get the rotten thing open. I'm also afraid that you'll have to excuse the mess.'

She led him through the French windows into a large room—a drawing room or parlour or music room or something of that nature. Whatever it was, it wasn't the kind of room he'd had much experience with and, despite her words, it wasn't ridiculously messy, but there were haphazard piles of boxes everywhere and piles of papers on the only piece of furniture in the room—a small side table.

'Why can't you get the door open?' He detached his arm from hers. Her warmth was…too warm.

'Oh, I don't know.' She waved a hand in the air. 'It's jammed or swollen up or something.'

Why hadn't she had it looked at?

None of your business. He hovered by the French windows until he heard the clang of the front gate closing behind the suit. He glanced behind to make sure anyway. He turned back to Nell. 'What was that all about?'

Those green eyes caught fire again. 'He's an estate agent who wants to sell my house, only I'm not interested. In more ways than one! He turned out to be a seriously sexist piece of work too. I can tell you now, Mr Bradford, that if you try any of the same tricks you'll meet with the same fate!'

She was a slim blonde firecracker. In a retro dress. He wanted to grin. And then he didn't.

The fire in her eyes faded. She made as if to wipe a hand down her face only she pulled it away at the last moment to clasp both her hands lightly in front of her.

She was so different from the last time he'd seen her.

'I'm sorry, that was an unforgivable thing to say. My blood's up and I'm not thinking clearly.'

'It's all right,' he said, because it was what he always said to a woman.

Nell shook her head. 'No, it's not. I have no right to tar you with the same brush as Mr Withers.'

That was when he noticed that behind the blonde princess perfection she had lines fanning out around her eyes and she wasn't wearing lipstick. 'I'd prefer it if you'd call me Rick.'

The hint of a smile played across her lips. 'Are you up for a coffee, Rick?'

And, just like that, she hurtled him back fifteen

years. *Come and play.* It hadn't been a demand or a request, but a plea.

He had to swallow the lump that came out of nowhere. He wanted to walk out of those French windows and never come back. He wanted...

He adjusted his stance. 'I thought you'd never ask.'

She smiled for real then and he realised that anything else that had passed for a smile so far hadn't reached her eyes. 'C'mon then.' She hitched her head and led him through the doorway into a hallway. 'You don't mind if we sit in the kitchen rather than the parlour, do you?'

'Not at all.' He tried to keep the wry note out of his voice. His type was never invited into the parlour.

Her shoulders tensed and he knew she'd read his tone. She wheeled around and led him in the other direction—back towards the front door—instead. She gestured into the large room to the left. 'As you'll see, the parlour is in a right state.'

He only meant to glance into the room but the sight dragged him all the way inside. In the middle of the room something huddled beneath dust sheets—probably furniture. It wasn't that which drew his attention. Plaster had fallen from one of the walls, adjacent to an ornate fireplace, and, while the mess had been swept up, nothing had been done about the gaping hole left behind. A rolled-up carpet leant against another wall along with more cardboard boxes. The light pouring in at the huge bay window did the room no favours either. Scratching sounded in the chimney. Birds or a possum?

He grimaced. 'A right state is the, uh, correct diagnosis'

'Yes, which is why I currently prefer the kitchen.'

Her voice might be crisp, but her shoulders weren't as straight as they could be. He followed her into the kitchen and then wasn't sure if it was much better. The housekeeper had obviously upped and left, but how long ago was anyone's guess. A jumble of dishes—mixing bowls and baking trays mostly—teetered in the sink, boxes of foodstuffs dominated one end of the enormous wooden table and flour seemed to be scattered over the rest of its surface. It smelt good in here, though.

She cleared a spot for him, wiped as much of the table down as she could and he sat. Mostly because it seemed the most sensible and least dangerous thing he could do. He didn't want to send anything flying with a stray elbow or a clumsy hip. Nell moved amid the mess with an ease and casual disregard as if she were used to it. He didn't believe that for a moment, though. The Princess had grown up in a world where others cleaned up the mess and kept things organised. This was merely a sign of her natural polish.

Or unnatural polish, depending on how one looked at it. She'd lacked it as a ten-year-old, but her parents had obviously managed to eventually drill it into her.

The scent of coffee hit him and he drew it slowly into his lungs. 'So…you're moving out?'

Nell started as if she'd forgotten he was there. She sent him one of those not quite smiles. 'Moving in, actually.'

Moving in? On her own? In this great old empty mansion?

None of your business.

His lips twisted. Since when had he been able to resist a damsel in distress? Or, in this case, a Princess in distress. 'What's going down, Nell?'

She turned fully to stare at him and folded her arms. 'Really?'

He wasn't sure what that *really* referred to—his genuine interest or his front in asking a personal question. He remembered his devil-may-care insolence and shrugged it on. 'Sure.'

She made coffee and set a mug in front of him. Only when he'd helped himself to milk and two sugars did she seat herself opposite and add milk to her own mug. The perfect hostess. The perfect princess.

'I'm sorry. I'm so used to everyone knowing my business that your question threw me for a moment.'

'I've only been back in town for a fortnight.' And he and she came from two different worlds, even if they had grown up in the same suburb.

Even amid all the disrepair and mess, she shone like some golden thing. Him? He just blended in.

'I did hear,' he ventured, 'that your father had fallen on hard times.'

Her lips tightened. 'And nearly took the livelihoods of over a hundred people with him in the process.'

Was she referring to the workers at the glass factory? It'd been in the Smythe-Whittaker family for three generations. Tash had told him how worried they'd been at the time that it'd go down the proverbial gurgler, that more unemployment would hit the area. But... 'I heard a buyer came in at the last minute.'

'Yes. No thanks to my father.'

'The global financial crisis has hit a lot of people hard.'

'That is true.' He didn't know why, but he loved the way she enunciated every syllable. 'However, rather than face facts, my father held on for so long that the sale of the factory couldn't cover all of his growing debts. I handed over the contents of my trust fund.'

Ouch.

'But I've drawn the line at selling Whittaker House.'

Her grandmother had left it to Nell rather than her father? Interesting. 'But you gave him your money?'

She rested both elbows on the table and stared down into her mug. 'Not all of it. I'd already spent some of it setting up my own business. Though, to be perfectly frank with you, Rick, it never really felt like my money. Besides, as I was never the daughter my father wanted, it seemed the least I could do.'

'But you're still angry with him.'

She laughed then and he liked the way humour curved her lips in that deliciously enticing manner. Lips like that didn't need lipstick. 'I am. And as everyone else around here already knows the reason, I'll even share it with you, tough guy.'

He leaned towards her, intrigued.

'Besides the fact he had no right gambling with the factory workers' livelihoods, his first solution was to marry me off to Jeremy Delaney.'

His jaw dropped. 'Jeez, Nell, the Delaneys might be rolling in it, but it's a not-so-secret secret that he's…' He trailed off, rolling his shoulders. Maybe Nell didn't know.

'Gay?' She nodded. 'I know. I don't know why he refuses to be loud and proud about it. I suspect he's still too overawed by his father.'

'And you refused to marry him?'

'Of course I did.'

He flashed back to the way she'd frogmarched the suit out of her office earlier and grinned. 'Of course you did.'

'So then my father demanded I sell this house.'

It wasn't a house—it was a mansion. But he refrained from pointing that out. 'And you refused to do that too?'

She lifted her chin. 'As everyone knows, I gave him the deeds to my snazzy little inner city apartment. I handed over my sports car and I signed over what was left of my trust fund, but I am not selling this house.' Her eyes flashed.

He held up his hands. 'Fair enough. I'm not suggesting you should. But jeez, Nell, if you don't have a cent left how are you going to afford its upkeep?'

The fire in her eyes died and her luscious lips drooped at the corners. And then he watched in amazement as she shook herself upright again. 'Cupcakes,' she said, her chin at *just* that angle.

'Cupcakes?' Had she gone mad?

In one fluid movement she rose, reached for a plate before pulling off a lid from a nearby tin. 'Strawberries and Cream, Passion Fruit Delight, Lemon Sherbet, and Butterscotch Crunch.' With each designation she pulled forth an amazing creation from the tin and set it onto the plate, and somehow the cluttered old kitchen was transformed into a…fairyland, a birthday party.

She set the plate in front of him with a flourish and all he could do was stare in amazement at four of the prettiest cupcakes he'd ever seen in his life.

'I do cupcake towers as birthday or special event cakes in whatever flavour or iced in whatever colour the client wants. I provide cupcakes by the dozen for birthday parties, high teas, morning teas and office parties. I will even package up an individual cupcake in a fancy box with all the bells and whistles…or, at least, ribbons and glitter, if that's what a client requests.'

He stared at the cakes on the plate in front of him

and then at the mountain of dishes in the sink. 'You made these? You?'

His surprise didn't offend her. She just grinned a Cheshire cat grin. 'I did.'

The Princess could bake?

She nodded at the cupcakes and handed him a bread and butter plate and a napkin. 'Help yourself.'

Was she serious? Guys like him didn't get offered mouth-watering treasures like these. Guys like him feigned indifference to anything covered in frosting or cream, as if a sweet tooth were a sign of a serious weakness.

He didn't stop to think about it; he reached for the nearest cupcake, a confection of sticky pale yellow frosting with a triangle of sugared lemon stuck in at a jaunty angle and all pale golden goodness, and then halted. He offered the plate to her first.

She glanced at her watch and shook her head. 'I'm only allowed to indulge after three p.m. and it's only just gone two.'

'That sounds like a stupid rule.'

'You don't understand. I find them addictive. For the sake of my hips and thighs and overall general health, I've had to put some limits to my indulging.'

He laughed and took a bite.

Moist cake, a surge of sweetness and the tang of lemon hit him in a rush. He closed his eyes and tried to stamp the memory onto his senses and everything inside him opened up to it. When he'd been in jail he'd occasionally tried to take himself away from the horror by imagining some sensory experience from the outside world. Small things like the rush of wind in his face as he skateboarded down a hill, the buoyancy of swimming in the ocean, the smell of wattle and eucalyptus in the national park. He'd have added the taste of the Princess's cupcakes if he'd experienced them way back when.

He finished the cupcake and stared hungrily at the plate. Would she mind if he had another one?

Rick stared at the three remaining cupcakes with so much hunger in his eyes that something inside Nell clenched up. It started as a low-level burn in her chest, but the burn intensified and hardened to eventually settle in her stomach. It was one thing to feel sorry for herself for the predicament she found herself in, but she'd never experienced the world as the harsh, ugly place Rick had. *And you'll do well not to forget it.*

She had to swallow before she could speak. 'Scoff the lot.' She pushed the plate closer. 'They're leftovers from the orders I delivered earlier.'

He glanced at her and the uncertainty in his eyes knifed into her. He'd swaggered in here with his insolent bad-boy cockiness set off to perfection in that tight black T-shirt, but it was just as much a show, a fake, as her society girl smile. Still… She glanced at those shoulders and her mouth watered.

In the next instant she shook herself. She did *not* find that tough-guy look attractive.

He pushed the plate away, and for some reason it made her heart heavy. So heavy it took an effort to keep it from sinking all the way to her knees.

'How…when did you learn to cook?'

She didn't want to talk about that. When she looked too hard at the things she was good at—cooking and gardening—and the reasons behind them, it struck her as too pathetic for words.

And she wasn't going to be pathetic any more.

So she pasted on her best society girl smile—the one she used for the various charity functions she'd always felt honour-bound to attend. 'It appears I have a natural aptitude for it.' She gave an elegant shrug. She knew it was elegant because she'd practised it endlessly until her mother could find no fault with it. 'Who'd have thought? I'm as surprised as everyone else.'

He stared at her and she found it impossible to read his expression. Except to note that the insolent edge had returned to his smile. 'What time did you start baking today?'

'Three a.m.'

Both of his feet slammed to the ground. He leant towards her, mouth open.

'It's Sunday, and Saturdays and Sundays are my busiest days. Today I had a tower cake for a little girl's birthday party, four dozen cupcakes for a charity luncheon, a hen party morning tea and a couple of smaller afternoon teas.'

'You did that all on your own?'

She tried not to let his surprise chafe at her. Some days it still shocked the dickens out of her too.

His face tightened and he glanced around the kitchen. 'I guess it does leave you the rest of the week to work on this place.'

Oh, he was just like everyone else! He thought her a helpless piece of fluff without a backbone, without a brain and probably without any moral integrity either. *You're useless.*

She pushed her shoulders back. 'I guess,' she said, icing-sugar-sweet, 'that all I need to do is find me a big strong man with muscles and know-how... and preferably with a pot of gold in the bank...to wrap around my little finger and...' She trailed off with another shrug—an expansive one this time. She traded in a whole vocabulary of shrugs.

A glint lit his eye. 'And then you'll never have to bake another cupcake again?'

'Ah, but you forget. I like baking cupcakes.'

'And getting up at three a.m.?'

She ignored that.

He frowned. 'Is that why you wanted to see me?'

It took a moment to work out what he meant. When she did, she laughed. 'I guess you have the muscles, but do you have the know-how?' She didn't ask him about the pot of gold. That would be cruel. 'Because I'm afraid I don't.' She bit back a sigh. *No self-pity.* 'But no, that's not why I asked you to drop by.'

His face hardened. 'So why did I receive the summons? If you knew I was at Tash's, why couldn't you have dropped by there?'

She heard what he didn't say. *Why do you think you're better than me?* The thing was, she didn't. He wouldn't believe that, though. She moistened her lips. 'I didn't think I'd be welcome there. I don't believe Tash thinks well of me.'

He scowled. 'What on earth—?'

'A while back I went into the Royal Oak.' It was the hotel where Tash worked. Nell had been lonely and had wanted to connect with people she'd never been allowed to connect with before. For heaven's sake, they all lived in the same neighbourhood. They should know each other. She was careful to keep the hurt out of her voice. She'd had a lot of practice at that too.

There you go again, feeling sorry for yourself.

She lifted her chin. 'I ordered a beer. Tash poured me a lemon squash and made it clear it'd be best for all concerned if I drank it and left.'

Rick stared at her, but his face had lost its frozen closeness. 'And you took that to mean she didn't like you?'

She had no facility for making friends and the recent downturn in her circumstances had only served to highlight that. 'Yes, I did.'

'Princess, I—'

'I really wish you wouldn't call me that.' She'd never been a princess, regardless of what Rick thought. 'I much prefer Nell. And there's absolutely no reason at all why Tash should like me.' Given the way her parents had ensured that Nell hadn't associated with the local children, it was no wonder they'd taken against her. Or that those attitudes had travelled with them into adulthood.

He looked as if he wanted to argue so she continued—crisp, impersonal, untouchable. 'Do you recall the gardener who worked here for many years?'

He leant back, crossed a leg so his ankle rested on his knee. Despite the casual demeanour, she could see him turning something over in his mind. 'He was the one who chased me away that day?'

That day. She didn't know how that day could still be so vivid in her mind. 'Come and play.' She'd reached out a hand through the eight-foot-high wrought iron fence and Rick had clasped it briefly before John had chased him off. John had told her that Rick wasn't the kind of little boy she should be playing with. But she'd found an answering loneliness in the ten-year-old Rick's eyes. It had given her the courage to speak to him in the first place. Funnily enough, even though Rick had only visited twice more, she'd never felt quite so alone again.

That day John had given her her very own garden bed. That had helped too.

But Rick remembered that day as well? Her heart started to pound though she couldn't have explained why. 'Yes, John was the one who chased you away.'

'John Cox. I remember seeing him around the

place. He drank at the Crown and Anchor, if memory serves me. Why? What about him?'

'Did you know him well?'

'I'm not sure I ever spoke to the man.'

'Right.' She frowned. Then this just didn't make any sense.

'Why?' The word barked out of him. 'What has he been saying?'

'Nothing.' She swallowed. 'He died eight months ago. Lung cancer.'

Rick didn't say anything and, while he hadn't moved, she sensed that his every muscle was tense and poised.

'John and I were…well, friends of a kind, I guess. I liked to garden and he taught me how to grow things and how to keep them healthy.'

'Cooking *and* gardening? Are your talents endless, Princess?'

She should've become immune to mockery by now, but she hadn't. She and Rick might've shared a moment of kinship fifteen years ago, but they didn't have anything in common now. That much was obvious. And she'd long given up begging for friends.

She gave a shrug that was designed to rub him up the wrong way, in the same way his 'Princess' was designed to needle her. A superior shrug that said *I'm better than you*. Her mother had been proficient at those.

Rick's lip curled.

She tossed her hair back over her shoulder. 'John

kept to himself. He didn't have many friends so I was one of the few people who visited him during his final weeks.'

Rick opened his mouth. She readied herself for something cutting, but he closed it again instead. She let out a breath. Despite what Rick might think of her, she'd cried when John had died. He'd been kind to her and had taken the time to show her how to do things. He'd answered her endless questions. And he'd praised her efforts. The fingers she'd been tapping on her now cold coffee cup stopped.

'Nell?'

She dragged herself back from those last days in John's hospice room. 'If the two of you never spoke, then what I'm about to tell you is rather odd, but…'

'But?'

She met his gaze. 'John charged me with a final favour.'

'What kind of favour?'

'He wanted me to deliver a letter.'

Dark brown eyes stared back at her, the same colour as dark chocolate. Eighty per cent cocoa. Bitter chocolate.

'He wanted me to give that letter to you, Rick.'

'To me?'

She rose and went to the kitchen drawer where she kept important documents. 'He asked that I personally place it in your hands.'

And then she held it out to him.

CHAPTER TWO

EVERY INSTINCT RICK had urged him to leap up and leave the room, to race out of this house and away from this rotten city and to never return.

He wanted away from Nell and her polished blonde perfection and her effortless nose-in-the-air superiority that was so at odds with the girl he remembered.

Fairy tales, that was what those memories were. He'd teased them out into full-blown fantasies in an effort to dispel some of the grim reality that had surrounded him. He'd known at the time that was what he'd been doing, but he'd wanted to hold up the promise of something better to come—a chance for a better future.

Of course, all of those dreams had shattered the moment he'd set foot inside a prison cell.

Still...

The letter in Nell's outstretched hand started to shake. 'Aren't you going to take it?'

'I'm not sure.'

She sat.

'I have no idea what this John Cox could have to say to me.' Did she know what was in the letter? He deliberately loosened his shoulders, slouched back in his chair and pasted on a smirk. 'Do you think he's going to accuse me of stealing the family silver?'

She flinched and just for a moment he remembered wild eyes as she ordered, 'Run!'

He wanted her to tell him to run now.

'After all, I didn't disappoint either his or your father's expectations.'

Those incredible eyes of hers flashed green fire and he wondered what she'd do next. Would she frogmarch him off the premises with his ear between her thumb and forefinger. And if she tried it would he let her? Or would he kiss her?

He shifted on the chair, ran a hand down his T-shirt. He wasn't kissing the Princess.

'If memory serves me correctly—' she bit each word out '—you went to jail on drug charges, not robbery. *And* if the rumours buzzing about town are anything to go by, those charges are in the process of being dropped and your name cleared.'

Did she think that made up for fifteen months behind bars?

A sudden heaviness threatened to fell him. One stupid party had led to...

He dragged a hand down his face. Cheryl, at seventeen, hadn't known what she'd been doing, hadn't known the trouble that the marijuana she'd bought could get her into—could get them all into. She'd been searching for escape—escape from a sexually abusive father. He understood that, sympathised. The fear that had flashed into her eyes, though, when the police had burst in, her desperation—the desperation of someone who'd been betrayed again and again by people who were supposed to love her—it still plagued his nightmares.

His chest cramped. Little Cheryl who he'd known since she'd started kindergarten. Little Cheryl who he'd done his best to protect…and, when that hadn't been enough, who he'd tried to comfort. He hadn't known it then, but there wasn't enough comfort in the world to help heal her. *It hadn't been her fault.*

So he'd taken the blame for her. He'd been a much more likely candidate for the drugs anyway. At the age of eighteen he'd gone to jail for fifteen months. He pulled in a breath. In the end, though, none of it had made any difference. That was what really galled him.

Nell thrust out her chin. 'So drop the attitude and stop playing the criminal with me.'

It snapped him out of his memories and he couldn't have said why, but he suddenly wanted to smile.

'The only way to find out what John has to say is to open the letter.'

He folded his arms. 'What's it to you, anyway?'

'I made a promise to a dying man.'

'And now you've kept it.'

She leaned across, picked up his hand and slapped

the letter into it. She smelled sweet, like cupcakes. 'Now I've kept it.'

A pulse pounded inside him. Nell moved back. She moved right across to the other side of the kitchen and refilled their mugs from the pot kept warm by the percolator hotplate. But her sugar-sweet scent remained to swirl around him. He swallowed. He blinked until his vision cleared and he could read his name in black-inked capitals on the envelope. For some reason, those capitals struck him as ominous.

For heaven's sake, just open the damn thing and be done with it. It'd just be one more righteous citizen telling him the exact moment he'd gone off the rails, listing a litany of perceived injuries received— both imagined and in some cases real—and then a biting critique of what the rest of his life would hold if he didn't mend his ways.

The entire thing would take him less than a minute to read and then he could draw a line under this whole stupid episode. With a half-smothered curse he made deliberately unintelligible in honour of the Princess's upper class ears, he tore open the envelope.

Heaving out a breath, he unfolded the enclosed sheet of paper. The letter wasn't long. At least he wouldn't have to endure a detailed rant. He registered when Nell placed another mug of coffee in front of him that she even added milk and sugar to it.

He opened his mouth to thank her, but…

The words on the page were in the same odd style

of all capitals as the envelope. All in the same black ink. He read the words but couldn't make sense of them to begin with.

They began to dance on the page and then each word rose up and hit him with the force of a sledgehammer. He flinched. He clenched the letter so hard it tore. He swore—loud and rude and blue—as black dots danced before his eyes.

Nell jumped. He expected her to run away. He told himself he hoped she would.

'Rick!' Her voice and its shrillness dive-bombed him like a magpie hostile with nesting instinct. 'Stick your head between your knees. Now!'

And then she was there, pushing his head between his knees and ordering him to breathe, telling him how to do it. He followed her instructions—pulling air into his lungs, holding it there and releasing it—but as soon as the dizziness left him he surged upright again.

He spun to her and waved the balled-up letter beneath her nose. 'Do you know what this says? Do you know what the—'

He pulled back the ugly language that clawed at his throat. 'Do you know what this says?' he repeated.

She shook her head. 'I wasn't there when he wrote it. It was already sealed when he gave it to me. He never confided in me about its contents and I never asked.' She gave one of *those* shrugs. 'I'll admit to a passing curiosity.' She drew herself up, all haughty blonde sleekness in her crazy, beautiful Hawaiian dress. 'But I would never open someone else's mail. So, no, I haven't read its contents.'

He wasn't sure he believed her.

She moved back around the table, sat and brought her mug to her lips. It was so normal it eased some of the raging beast inside him.

She glanced up, her eyes clouded. 'I do hope he hasn't accused you of something ridiculous like stealing my grandmother's pearls.'

He sat too. 'It's nothing like that.'

'Good, because I know for a fact that was my father.'

He choked. *Father*. The word echoed through his mind. Father. Father. *Father*. In ugly black capitals.

'And I'm sorry I've not tracked you down sooner to give that letter to you, but John died and then my father's business fell apart and…and I wasn't sure where to look for you.'

He could see now that she hadn't wanted to approach Tash to ask how she might find him.

He wasn't sorry. Not one little bit.

'But when I heard you were home…'

He dragged a hand down his face before gulping half his coffee in one go. 'Did he say anything else to you when he gave you this?' The letter was still balled in his hand.

She reached out as if to swipe her finger through the frosting of one of the cupcakes, but she pulled her hand back at the last moment. 'He said you might have some questions you'd like to ask me and that he'd appreciate it if I did my best to answer them.'

He coughed back a hysterical laugh. Some questions? All he had were questions.

Her forehead creased. 'This isn't about that nonsense when we were ten-year-olds, is it?'

He didn't understand why she twisted her hands together. She wasn't the one who'd been hauled to the police station.

'I tried to tell my parents and the police that I gave the locket to you of my own free will and that you hadn't taken it. That I gave it to you as a present.'

She stared down into her coffee and something in her face twisted his gut.

'I thought it was mine to give.' She said the words so softly he had to strain to catch them. He thought about how she'd handed her apartment, her car and her trust fund all over to her father without a murmur. So why refuse to hand over Whittaker House?

She straightened and tossed back her hair. 'That was the moment when I realised my possessions weren't my own.'

But for some reason she felt that Whittaker House was hers?

'I told them how I wanted to give you something because you'd given me your toy aeroplane.'

It was the only thing he'd had to give her.

'Which, mind you, I absolutely refused to hand over when they demanded me to.'

That made him laugh.

She met his gaze squarely and there wasn't an ounce of haughtiness in her face. He sobered. 'I've never had the chance to say it before but, Rick, I'm sorry. My mother and father were so angry. And then the policeman frightened me so much I...I eventually just told them what they wanted to hear. It was cowardly of me and I'm truly sorry if that episode caused a lot of trouble for you.'

It'd caused trouble all right. It was the first time he'd come to the police's attention. It hadn't been the last time he'd been labelled a thief, liar and trouble-maker by them, though.

They'd just been two kids exchanging treasures and trying to forge a connection. Her father, the police and his background had all conspired to blow it out of proportion.

But none of it had been Nell's fault and he'd always known that. 'Don't sweat it, Princess.' He used the nickname to remind himself of all the differences between them, to reinforce them.

She sat back, her chin tilted at that unconsciously noble angle that made him want to smile. 'Don't worry. I was let off with a caution, but I didn't know the police had questioned you too.' The poor kid had probably been terrified. He had been.

She nodded to the letter balled in his hand. 'But John hasn't hassled you about any of that?'

He shook his head and her shoulders slumped in relief. She straightened again a moment later. 'So... do you have any questions?'

She looked as puzzled and bewildered as he felt. He wondered if she was counting down the minutes until this interview ended. Did she find it awkward and wrong for him to be sitting across the table from her? Or did it feel weirdly comfortable?

He shook off the thought and set the crumpled letter on the table and did what he could to smooth it out.

'*I won't beat around the bush*,' he read, '*but you might as well know that I'm your father.*'

Nell's mug wobbled back to the table. She stared at him. Her mouth opened and closed. 'But he chased you away.' And then her eyes filled.

Rick knew then that she'd had no notion of what John's letter contained.

He glanced back at the letter and continued reading. '*I may be better served taking this knowledge to the grave as it's brought me no joy. I don't expect it to bring you any either.*'

Nell's intake of breath reverberated in the silence.

'*I have no faith in you.*'

Her hands slapped to the table.

'*But you might as well know you have a sibling.*'

She practically leapt out of her chair. 'Who?' she demanded, and then forced herself back down into her seat. 'Really?' She frowned. 'Older or younger?'

He raised an eyebrow. 'I think I'm the one who's supposed to be asking the questions.'

'Oh, yes, of course.' She sat back and folded her hands in her lap. 'I'm sorry.'

'*I'm not going to tell you who it is. If it matters to you then you'll have to prove it.*'

Her jaw dropped. 'But that's… How…how can he be so hard and cold? He's supposed to have looked after you and…' She swallowed and sat back again. 'Sorry.' She smiled, a weak thing that did nothing to hide her turmoil. She made a zipping motion across her mouth.

Rick shrugged. 'He ends by simply signing it *John Cox.*'

She shook herself, frowned. 'I know the questions belong to you, but, Rick, I have no idea how to answer any of them. I haven't a clue who your sibling could be. I had no idea John was your father. I've never seen him with either a woman or a child. I—'

He handed the letter to her. He watched her face as she read the remaining lines. It darkened, which gladdened his heart.

And then it went blank. Rick eased back in his chair and stared up at the ceiling, not knowing whether to be relieved or disappointed.

Nell ignored the first lines John addressed to her in the letter. *Miss Nell, if you think Rick is in any way redeemable and you can find it in yourself to help him…* She snorted. What kind of nonsense was that? What kind of father just turned his back on his child? She thought about her own father with all of his demands and bit back a sigh.

'*You'll find a clue where the marigolds grow.*' She

turned the letter over, but there was nothing written on the back.

'Any idea what that might mean?' Rick asked, slouching back in his chair as if they were discussing nothing more interesting than the weather.

She opened her mouth. She closed it again and scratched her head. 'My best guess is that, as he was a gardener and this is where he gardened, it refers to a garden bed somewhere on the estate, a garden bed where he grew marigolds, but...'

'But?'

Rick sounded bored. She glanced at him, tried to read his face, but couldn't. She lifted one shoulder. 'The thing is, I don't recall John ever growing marigolds. Apparently my mother didn't like them.'

She stabbed a finger into the Passion Fruit Delight cupcake, glowering at it. 'Why couldn't he have just told you who your sibling is?' She stabbed it again. 'Why couldn't he have told you the truth from the start and been a proper father to you?' Stab. Stab. 'I'd never have guessed any of this in a million years and—'

She pulled herself up and collected herself. None of this was helping. She wiped her finger on a napkin. 'Okay, so what else could marigold mean?'

Rick picked up the Strawberries and Cream cupcake and pushed nearly half of it into his mouth. She watched, mesmerised, at the way his lips closed around it, at the appreciation that lit his eyes and the way his mouth worked, the way his Adam's apple bobbed…the way his tongue flicked out to seize a crumb from the corner of his mouth.

She wrenched her gaze back. 'It could be a girl's name.' Her voice came out strangled.

'Do you know a Marigold or two?'

The words came out lazy and barely interested. Didn't he care? She tried to focus on the question he asked rather than the ones pounding through her. She frowned, thought hard and eventually shook her head. 'I don't think so. I don't even think I know any Marys.' She leapt up, seized her address book from the sideboard drawer and flicked through it… and then searched the list of contacts in her mobile phone. Nothing.

She stood. 'Okay, maybe there's marigold wallpaper somewhere in the house or…or moulding in the shape of a marigold…or an ornament or a painting or—'

'Princess, you've lived here your whole life. Do you really need to go through this mausoleum room by room to know whether it has marigold wallpaper?'

No, of course not. She sat. She knew every room intimately. She could remember what it looked like ten years ago as if it were only yesterday. There hadn't been any marigold paintings on any of the walls. There'd been no marigold wallpaper or bedspreads or curtains. No marigolds. Anywhere.

She glanced at Rick again. She could deal with his devil-may-care teasing and that tough-guy swagger.

In fact, those things gave her a bit of a thrill. Considering she didn't get too many thrills, she'd take them where she could. She could even deal with the cold, hard wall he retreated behind. She could relate to it, even if she did feel he was judging her behind it and finding her lacking. But this… This nothingness hidden behind mockery and indifference. She was having no part of it.

She folded her arms. 'Don't you care?'

'Why should I?' He licked his fingers clean.

'Because…'

'What did he ever do for me?'

'Not about John!' She could understand his indifference and resentment of the other man. On that head it was John's stance that baffled her. She leaned across the table until its edges dug into her ribs. 'Don't you care that you have a brother or sister somewhere in the wide world?'

One shoulder lifted. He reached for the last unmangled cupcake. A dark lick of hair fell across his forehead. Nell pushed away from the table to stare, unseeing, out of the kitchen window, determined not to watch him demolish it with those delectable lips, determined not to watch him demolish it the way he seemed hell-bent on destroying this chance, this gift, he'd been given.

She pressed her hands to her chest. To have a sibling…

She stilled. She glanced back behind her for a second and then spun back. Rick *hadn't* left. He hadn't read John's letter and then stormed out. He *had* shared the letter with her. Rick could feign indifference and couldn't-care-less disregard all he wanted, but if he really didn't care he'd have left by now.

Her cupcakes were good, but they weren't that good.

She sat again. 'I wish I had a brother or sister.'

'And whose image would you most like them cast in?' He leaned back, hands clasped behind his head. 'Your mother's or your father's?'

She flinched. He blinked and for a moment she thought he might reach across the table to touch her. He didn't. She forced herself to laugh. 'I guess there is always that. A sibling may have provided further proof that I was the cuckoo in the nest.'

'I didn't mean it like that.'

The hell he hadn't. 'It's okay.' She made her voice wry. 'You've had a shock, so it's okay to say hurtful things to other people.'

He scrubbed a hand across his face. 'I didn't mean for it to be hurtful. I'm sorry. I just refuse to turn this into a "they-all-lived-happily-ever-after" fairy tale like you seem so set on doing.'

He didn't want to get his hopes up. She couldn't blame him for that.

He rose. 'I believe I've long outstayed my welcome.'

Nell shot to her feet too. 'But…but we haven't figured out what marigolds mean yet or—'

'I'm not sure I care, Princess.'

She opened her mouth, but he shook his head and the expression on his face had her shutting it again. 'Good girl,' he said.

Her chin shot up. 'Don't patronise me.'

He grinned a grin that made her blood heat and her knees weak and she suddenly wanted him gone. Now. 'You know where to find me if you decide to investigate this issue further.' And then she swung away to dump the used coffee grounds into the kitchen tidy. When she turned back he was gone. She sat, her heart pounding as if she'd run a race.

Rick let himself into Tash's house, his head whirling and his temples throbbing. What the hell was he supposed to do now?

What do you want to do?

He wanted to run away.

But...

He pulled up short, dragged in a breath and searched for his customary indifference, but he couldn't find it. Too many thoughts pounded at him. And one hard, implacable truth—he might not be able to do anything with the information John Cox had belatedly decided to impart. Marigolds might remain unsolved forever.

In which case he could jump in his car—*now*— and head north without a backward glance, without a single regret. Except...

What if Nell does work out what it means?

He had a brother or a sister. He rested his hands against his knees and tried to breathe through the fist that tightened around his chest.

'That you, Rick?'

Tash's voice hauled him upright. 'Yep, just me,' he called back, shoving aside the worst of his anger and confusion. Tash might be his best friend, but he wasn't sharing this news with anyone.

He just hoped the Princess would keep her mouth shut too.

He forced his feet down the hallway and into Tash's living room—still full of sun and summer, and all he wanted to do was close his eyes and sleep. One glance at him and Tash's eyes narrowed. 'What did Nell want?'

He swung away to peer into the fridge. 'Soda?'

'No, thanks.'

He grabbed a soda and then sauntered over to plant himself in an armchair.

Tash folded her arms. 'She's obviously pushed your buttons.'

'Nah, not really.' He shrugged. 'She wanted to know if I had the time and the inclination to do some work on Whittaker House.'

'Oh, Lord, you're going to make the Princess your next project?'

He stretched out a leg. 'I haven't decided yet.' He took a long drink. The cold liquid helped ease the burning in his throat. 'Mind you, the place is going to rack and ruin.'

'It's a shame. It's such a nice old place. Gossip has it that she only moved back in this week so she's not wasting any time getting things shipshape again.' Tash sent him one of her looks. 'Rumour has it that she's far from cash-happy at the moment.'

'I kinda got that impression. What else does rumour say?'

Tash managed a local pub—The Royal Oak. Lots of workers from the glass factory drank there. What Tash didn't know about local happenings wasn't worth knowing.

'Well, apparently there's no love lost between Nell and her father.'

She could say that again.

'Old Mrs Smythe-Whittaker left the house to Nell and I'm not sure how these things work, but it was left in trust for her father to manage until Nell turned twenty-five.' Tash's lips twisted. 'Nell turned twenty-five earlier in the week. She moved in and...'

'Her father moved out?'

'Bingo.'

Before he could ask any more, Mitch came striding into the room. 'Hey, gorgeous.'

'Hey, doll,' Rick murmured back, but neither Tash nor Mitch paid him the slightest attention.

Tash flew out of her chair to launch herself at the big blond detective. 'Catch any bad guys today?'

Mitch thrust out his chest and pounded on it with one hand. 'Loads.'

For a moment it made Rick grin. Mitch the shrewd

detective and Tash the take-no-prisoners barmaid in love and flirting. A miracle of miracles.

He rose and set off back down the hallway for the front door. 'I'm eating out tonight,' he tossed over his shoulder.

He needed time to think.

He pushed out of the front door, his hand clenching into a fist. This whole thing could be an elaborate hoax, a nasty trick.

Or you could have a brother or a sister.

Could he really walk away from this?

He lengthened his stride but the thoughts and confusion continued to bombard him. Damn it all to hell! Why did this have to involve the Princess? She'd been trouble fifteen years ago and hard-won wisdom warned him she'd be trouble now.

There was something about her that set his teeth on edge too.

Somewhere inside him a maniacal laugh started up.

The next afternoon, Nell swiped a forearm across her brow and stared at the mountain of dishes that needed washing.

Staring at them won't get them done. If she were going to take a half-day on Mondays then she needed to use that time productively. She started to move towards them when a knock sounded on the back door.

She spun around and then swallowed. Rick. In worn jeans and another tight black T-shirt. And with that bad-boy insolence wrapped tightly around him. She didn't know whether to be relieved or something altogether different—like apprehensive.

She wiped her hands down her shorts. Instinct warned her that the less time she spent in Rick's company the better. Better for her peace of mind and better for her health if the stupid way her heart leapt and surged was anything to go by. She tried to swallow back her misgivings. Her family had done this man no favours. She owed him for that.

With a sigh she waved him inside, kissing good-bye to the notion of a clean kitchen followed by a soak in a hot tub with a good book. 'Good afternoon.'

He just nodded as he took the same seat at the table as he had the previous day.

'Can I get you anything?'

'No, thanks.'

Neither of them spoke and the silence grew heavy. Nell moistened her lips. 'I…' She couldn't think of anything to say.

Rick's gaze speared to hers. 'Shall I tell you what occurred to me overnight?'

Her mouth dried though she couldn't have explained why. She gave a *please continue* shrug.

'I wondered if there was the slightest possibility that by staying here it meant John Cox had the chance to remain close to his other child?'

It took a moment for that inference to sink in. In a twisted way, she could see how he could make that leap. Without a word she went to her important documents drawer and pulled out a folder. She opened her mouth to try and explain its contents only to snap it shut. She shoved the folder at Rick instead. The contents could speak for themselves.

He stared at her for a moment and then riffled through the enclosed sheaf of papers. A frown lowered over his face even as his chin lifted. For a moment he looked like a devil. One who'd cajole with dark temptations that could only end in destruction and ruin. Her heart kicked in her chest.

She swallowed and looked away.

'This is a paternity test your father had done… twelve years ago.'

'That's correct. He arranged for that test when he and my mother divorced. As he said at the time, he had no intention of being financially responsible for a child that wasn't his.' Only the tests had shown beyond a shadow of a doubt that she was his daughter.

And that he was her father.

Rick slammed the folder shut. 'God, Nell, that man's a nightmare of a father!'

She turned back and raised an eyebrow. 'Snap.'

He rocked back and then a grin crept across those fascinating lips of his and a light twinkled in those dark eyes and some of the awkwardness between them seeped away. 'Okay, you got me there. I'll pay that.'

And then he laughed, and the laugh completely transformed him. It tempered the hard, insolent edges and made him look young and carefree. It made him breathtakingly attractive too, in a dangerous, thrilling way that had her blood surging and her pulse pounding.

She swallowed. 'On that head, though…' She nodded at the folder. 'I can't say I blame him. My mother isn't the kind of woman who has ever let the truth get in the way of a…good opportunity.'

Her mother was in the Mediterranean with husband number four the last she'd heard, which was about three times a year. Oh, yes, her family—they were the Brady Bunch all right.

Rick clasped his hands behind his head and leaned back. She wondered if he knew precisely how enticing that pose was to a woman—the broad shoulders on display, those biceps and the hard chiselled chest flagrantly defined in the tight black T-shirt angling down to a hard flat abdomen…and all in that deceptively open, easy, inviting posture.

She bet he did.

Even with all of that masculine vigour on display, it was his eyes that held her. He surveyed her until she had to fight the urge to fidget. She reached for another shrug—a *pray tell, what on earth do you think you're staring at?* shrug. She was pretty certain she pulled it off with aplomb, but it didn't stop him staring at her. A ghost of a smile touched his lips. 'I'm starting to get the hang of those.'

She squinted at him—a *what on earth are you talking about?* squint. 'I'm sorry, you've lost me.'

He lowered his arms. 'For all of these years, here I was thinking you had the best of everything.'

She flicked her hair over her shoulders. 'Of course I did. I had the best education money could buy. I had designer clothes, piano lessons and overseas holidays. I had—'

'Parents who were as good at parenting as mine.'

She swallowed. 'One shouldn't be greedy.' Or self-pitying. 'Besides, they were merely products of their own upbringing…and they had their good points.'

'Name one.'

'We've already uncovered one. They didn't betray each other so badly that I was the cuckoo they thought I might be. I'm not John's secret love child and therefore I'm not your mystery sibling.'

'Just thought I'd ask.'

She hesitated. 'I did wonder…'

'What?'

'Would your mother be able to tell you anything that might be of use?'

She didn't like to ask about Rick's mother—she'd been a prostitute. Nell had a lot of bones to pick with her parents, but she'd never had to watch her mother sell her body. She'd always known where her next meal was coming from. She'd had a warm bed to retreat to. She'd been safe. She gripped her hands together. She was *very* grateful for those things.

Rick shook his head. 'She developed dementia a

few years ago. It's advanced rapidly. Nine times out of ten, she doesn't recognise me these days.'

Oh. Her heart burned for him. 'I'm sorry.'

He merely shrugged. 'What are you going to do?' He said it in that casual, offhand way, which only made her heart burn more fiercely.

She clapped her hands together in an attempt to brisk the both of them up. 'Well, I had another thought too. We should go and check out John's cottage. It's been empty since he went into hospital. I mean, I know it was cleaned, but maybe it'll contain some clue.'

'It could all be a hoax, you know?'

'For what purpose?' She didn't believe it was a hoax. Not for a moment. And when she made for the door, Rick rose and followed.

They picked their way through the overgrown garden—across the terrace to the lawn and then towards the far end of the block. Whittaker House had been built on generous lines in more generous times. The house and grounds sprawled over the best part of a city block. No wonder her father wanted her to sell it.

She wasn't selling! But it all needed so much attention. She bit back a sigh. It was all she could do not to let her heart slump with every step they took. It had all been so beautiful once upon a time.

'Hell, Princess, this looks more like years rather than months of neglect.'

'John was sick for a long time before he had to

go into the hospice. He had a young chap in to help him, but…' She shrugged and glanced around. Her father hadn't maintained any of it. 'There are a lot of vigorous-growing perennials here that have self-seeded and gone wild. It looks worse than it is.' She crossed her fingers.

'Do you see any self-seeding marigolds?'

He'd adopted that tone again. 'I'm afraid marigolds are annuals not perennials. They need to be replanted each year.'

'Why go to all that bother?'

'For the colour and spectacular blooms. For the scents and the crazy beauty of it all. Because—'

She slammed to a halt and Rick slammed right into the back of her. 'What on earth—'

He grabbed her shoulders to steady her, but she didn't need steadying. She spun around and gripped his forearms. '*You'll find a clue where the marigolds grow.*'

His face lost some of its cockiness. And a lot of its colour. She couldn't concentrate when he stared at her so intently. She sat on the edge of the nearest raised bed and rubbed her temples. 'When did I find out my mother didn't like marigolds? John told me when I wanted to plant some of my own.'

Rick sat beside her, crushing part of a rampant rosemary bush. The aroma drifted up around them.

'And why did I want to plant marigolds?' *Oh, but…* 'He couldn't have known, could he?'

'Couldn't have known what?'

She turned to him. 'After he chased you away that day he gave me my very own garden bed to tend.'

'And you grew marigolds?'

She shook her head. 'I wanted to, but I didn't. You see I had this old chocolate box tin and it had pictures of marigolds on it and I showed it to John and told him that's what I wanted to grow.'

Beside her, Rick stiffened. 'A tin?'

She nodded.

'What happened to the tin, Nell?'

'I put all of my treasures in it and...' But it had been a secret. John couldn't have known. Could he?

'What did you do with them?'

'I buried them here in the garden. After the policeman left. I snuck out in the middle of the night and buried them when nobody could see what I was up to.' She turned to meet his chocolate-dark eyes. 'And I never dug it back up.'

He swallowed. 'Okay, so all we have to do is try to find where you buried it.' He leaned back on his hands as if he hadn't a care in the world, but she'd seen beneath the façade now. 'I bet you've long forgotten that?'

No. She remembered. Perfectly.

She leaned back on her hands too, crushing more rosemary until the air was thick with its scent. She drew a breath of it into her lungs. 'Doesn't that remind you of a Sunday roast?'

He didn't say anything.

'What are you afraid of?' She asked the question

she had no right to ask. She asked because he kept calling her Princess and it unnerved her and she wanted to unnerve him back.

'Where I come from, Nell, Sunday roasts weren't just a rarity; they were non-existent.'

He said her name in a way that made her wish he'd called her Princess instead.

He leaned in towards her. 'And what am I afraid of? I'm afraid this isn't some hoax your gardener has decided to play and that everything he's said is true. I'm afraid I have a thirteen-year-old brother somewhere out there growing up by the scruff of his neck the way I did and with no one to give him a hand.'

Her stomach churned.

'I'm afraid he's going to end up in trouble. Or, worse, as a damn statistic.'

She pressed a hand to her stomach and her mouth went so dry she couldn't swallow.

'Is that good enough for you?'

It wasn't good. It was *horrible*. Her parents might not have been all that interested in her, but she hadn't been allowed to roam the streets unchecked or at risk of being taken advantage of. Her parents might not have been interested in her, but she had been protected.

'I remember exactly where I buried it, Rick.'

He stared and then he half laughed. 'You're full of surprises, aren't you?'

She leapt up and dusted off her shorts. 'We'd better hope John put it back in exactly the same spot or we're going to be spending a lot of time digging.'

She led the way to the garden shed. She grabbed a spade, secateurs and a couple of trowels. And gloves. Rick merely scoffed when she asked if he'd like a pair too. 'On your own head be it,' she warned. 'We're heading for the most overgrown part of the garden.'

He took the spade and secateurs before sweeping an elegant bow. 'Lead the way, Princess.'

It was crazy, but it made her feel like a princess. Not a princess on a pedestal, but a flesh and blood one.

She led him across to the far side of the garden. 'I'll trade you a trowel for the secateurs.' He handed them to her and she cut back canes from a wisteria vine gone mad. 'That's going to be a nightmare whenever I find the time to deal with it,' she grumbled. She cut some more so he had room to move in beside her. 'Believe it or not, there's a garden bed there.'

She trimmed the undergrowth around it, found the corners. It wasn't as big as she remembered, but that still didn't make it small.

She moved into the centre of it, stomping impatiens and tea roses. She closed her eyes and shuffled three steps to the right. She took a dolly step forward and drew an X on the ground. 'X marks the spot,' she whispered.

CHAPTER THREE

RICK STARED AT the spot and cold sweat prickled his nape. What the hell was he doing here?

To run now, though, would reveal weakness and he *never* showed weakness. In the world where he'd grown up weakness could prove fatal.

Not showing weakness and acting with strength, though, were two different things. When Nell took one of the trowels from his nerveless fingers, he couldn't do a damn thing about it. He couldn't move to help her. He couldn't ask her to stop.

'The spade will be overkill, I expect. The ground is soft and although it felt like I'd dug for a long time I was only ten so I expect the tin shouldn't be buried too deeply.'

It was only when she dropped to her knees in the dirt that Rick was able to snap back to himself. 'Princess, you'll get dirty.'

She grinned, but she didn't look up. 'I like getting mucky in the garden.'

She certainly knew how to wield a trowel.

'Cupcakes aren't the only things I'm good at, you know?'

'I didn't doubt for a moment that you'd be a gardening expert too.' He wondered if he should climb into the garden bed and help her. Except she looked so at home and he had a feeling he'd only get in the way. 'Can I help?'

Her grin widened. 'Nah, you just stand there and look pretty.'

He couldn't help it. He had to grin too.

'I can cook other things too. I'll cook you a Sunday roast some time and then you'll know what I meant about the scent of rosemary.'

Something hard and unbending inside him softened a fraction. Digging in the garden, grinning and teasing him, she was the antithesis of the haughty, superior woman she'd turned into yesterday. He could see now that he'd done something to trigger that haughtiness because Nell used her supercilious shrugs and stuck her nose in the air as a shield. The same way he used his devil-may-care grins and mocking eyebrows.

As he continued to stare at her, some parts of him might be softening, but other parts were doing the exact opposite. He adjusted his stance and concentrated on getting himself back on an even keel.

He wasn't letting a slip of a girl—any girl—knock him off balance.

'Princess, I admire cooking and gardening skills as much as the next man, but it's all very domestic goddessy.' A bit old-fashioned. He was careful to keep the judgement out of his voice and the mockery from his eyebrows. He didn't want her getting all hoity-toity again.

'Oh, that'd be because—'

She froze. It was only for a second but he was aware of every fraction of that second—the dismay on her face, the way the trowel trembled and then the stubborn jut of her jaw. She waved a hand in the air, dismissing the rest of whatever she'd been about to say.

He frowned. *What on earth...?*

Metal hitting metal made them both freeze. With a gulp, Nell continued digging. Rick collapsed onto the wooden sleeper that made the border for the bed and tried to ease the pounding in his chest.

Within a few moments Nell had freed the tin, brushed the dirt from its surface along with the dirt from her knees. She dropped the trowel at Rick's feet and settled herself beside him. The tin sat in her lap. They both stared at it as she pulled her hands free of the gloves. She reached out to trace the picture on the lid.

'Marigolds,' he said softly.

She nodded.

'Why didn't John let you plant marigolds here?'

'Because my mother didn't like them, remember?'

'Nobody would've seen them all the way down the back here.'

She lifted a shoulder. 'I found it was always best not to make waves if one could help it.'

'I decided on an opposite course of action.'

She glanced up with a grin, her green eyes alive with so much impish laughter it made his chest clench. 'You did at that. I'm going to take a leaf out of your book and fill this entire garden bed with marigolds.'

Good for her.

She held the tin out to him. 'Would you like to do the honours?'

His mouth went dry. He shook his head. 'They were your treasures.' He couldn't help adding, 'Besides, you could be wrong and maybe John never knew about the tin.'

'I'm not wrong.'

Her certainty had his heart beating hard and fast.

She sent him a small smile. 'Well, here goes.' And she prised the lid off.

An assortment of oddments met his gaze. Silly stuff one would expect a ten-year-old to treasure. And from it all she detached a small gold locket that he recognised immediately. She held it out to him and his heart gave a gigantic kick. 'When I buried this I swore that if I ever had the chance I'd give it to you.'

'Nell, I couldn't—'

She dropped it in his hand. 'Even now it brings me no joy. It reminds me of the trouble it caused. Throw it away if you want and spare me the bother.'

His hand closed about it and his heart thumped. In kid-speak their exchange of gifts had been a token of friendship. Not that the adults had seen it that way. But the locket shone as brilliantly for him now as it had back then.

'While I keep this.'

She held up the tin aeroplane he'd given her and a laugh broke from him. He took it from her and flew it through the air the way he used to do as a boy. 'You really did keep it.'

'I wasn't a defiant child. I generally did as I was told.' Her lips twisted. 'Or, at least, I tried to. This was the one thing I dug my heels in about.'

Along with this big old relic of a Victorian mansion. He wondered why it meant so much to her.

'I should've dug my heels in harder about the rest of it too, Rick. I'm sorry I didn't.'

He handed her back the plane. 'Forget about it. We were just kids.' And what chance did a timid ten-year-old have against bullying parents and glaring policemen?

'Hey, I remember those—' he laughed when she pulled out a host of cheap wire bangles in an assortment of garish colours '—the girls at school went mad for them for a while.'

'I know and I coveted them. I managed to sneak into a Two Dollar Shop and buy these when my mother wasn't looking, but she forbade me from wearing them. Apparently they made me look cheap and she threatened to throw them away.'

So instead Nell had buried them in this tin where no one could take them away from her…but where she'd never be able to wear them either. Not even in secret.

She dispensed quickly with a few other knick-knacks—some hair baubles and a Rubik's Cube—along with some assorted postcards. At the very bottom of the tin were two stark white envelopes. The writing on them was black-inked capitals.

One for Nell.

One for him.

With a, 'Tsk,' that robbed the moment of its ominousness, she handed them both to him and then proceeded to pile her 'treasures' back into the tin and eased the lid back on. 'Do we want to rip them open here or does it call for coffee?'

'Coffee?' His lip curled, although he tried to stop it.

'You're right. It's not too early for a drink, is it?'

'Hell, no. It has to be getting onto three o'clock.'

'I don't have any beer, but I do have half a bottle of cheap Chardonnay in the fridge.'

'Count me in.'

He carried the spade, the secateurs and the letters. She carried the trowels and the tin. It touched him that she trusted him with her letter. He could simply make off with both letters and try to figure out what game John Cox was playing at. But the gold locket burned a hole in his pocket and he knew he wasn't going anywhere.

Besides, Nell had been the one to decipher the clue and dig up the tin. So he helped her stow the garden tools and followed her across the weed-infested lawn, along the terrace and back into the kitchen. He set both letters onto the table. Nell washed her hands, collected two wine glasses and the bottle of wine.

He took the bottle, glanced at the label and grinned. 'You weren't joking when you said cheap, were you?'

'Shut up and pour,' she said cheerfully. 'When it's a choice between cheap wine and no wine…'

'Good choice,' he agreed, but a burn started up in his chest at all this evidence of the Princess fallen on hard times.

He handed her a glass, she clinked it with his and sat. He handed her the letter. She didn't bother with preliminaries. She set her glass down, tore open the envelope, and scanned the enclosed sheet of paper.

Rick remained standing, his heart thudding.

With a sound of disgust she thrust it at him. 'I don't like these games.'

Rick read it.

Dear Miss Nell,
If you think he's worth the effort, would you please pass these details on to him?
Yours sincerely,
John Cox.

She leapt up and snatched the letter back. 'He calls you "him" and "he's".' She slapped the sheet of paper with the back of her hand. 'He doesn't even have the courtesy to name you. It's…it's…'

'It's okay.'

She stared at him. She gave him back the letter. 'No, it's not.' She took her seat again and sipped her wine. She didn't grimace at its taste as he thought she would. In fact, she looked quite at home with her cheap wine. He'd have smiled except his letter burned a hole in his palm.

'And just so you know,' she added, 'the details there are for his solicitor.'

Rick didn't think for a moment that John had left him any money. It'd just be another hoop to jump through. Gritting his teeth, he slid a finger beneath the flap of the envelope addressed to him and pulled the letter free.

At least it was addressed to him.

Rick
If you've got this far then you have the approval of the only woman I've ever trusted and the only woman I have any time for. If you haven't blown it, she'll provide you with the information you'll need for the next step of the journey.

It was simply signed *John Cox*.

He handed the letter to Nell so she could read it

too. It seemed mean-spirited not to. She read it and handed it back. 'Loquacious, isn't he?'

Rick sank down into his chair.

'The solicitor, Clinton Garside, is wily and unpleasant.'

'Just like John Cox.'

She shook her head and then seemed to realise she was contradicting him. Based on all the evidence Rick had so far, 'wily and unpleasant' described John to a T. 'I never knew this side of him. He was quiet, didn't talk much and certainly wasn't affectionate, but he was kind to me.'

Maybe so, but he still hadn't let her plant marigolds.

Nell glanced at Rick and it suddenly hit her that he was only a step or two away from abandoning this entire endeavour.

She didn't know why, but instinct warned her that would be a bad thing—not bad evil, but bad detrimental. That it would hurt him in some fundamental way. As the messenger of the tidings she couldn't help feeling partly responsible.

You have enough troubles of your own.

Be that as it may. She owed Rick. She owed him for what had happened fifteen years ago. She owed him for letting herself be browbeaten, for not being strong enough to have defended him when that had been the right thing to do. She might only have been ten years old, but she'd known right from wrong. She had no intention of making the same mistake now.

She straightened. 'Clint will give you the run-around. He'll tell you he won't be able to see you for weeks, and that's not acceptable.'

'Nell, I—'

'If you have a sibling out there who needs you—' she fixed him with a glare '—then it's unacceptable.'

His lips pressed together in a tight line. He slumped back in his seat without another word.

Nell pulled her cellphone from her handbag and punched in Clint Garside's number. 'Hello, it's Nell Smythe-Whittaker. I'd like to make an appointment to see Mr Garside, please. I know he's very busy, but it's rather important and I was hoping to meet with him as soon as possible.'

'I'll just check his appointment book,' the receptionist said.

'Thank you, I appreciate that.' She searched her mind and came back with a name. 'Is that you, Lynne?'

'It is, Ms Smythe-Whittaker.'

'Please, call me Nell. How's your husband coming along after his football injury? Will he be right to play the first game of the season? All the fans are hoping so.'

'We think so, fingers crossed. It's nice of you to ask.'

Exactly. And in return…

'There's just been a cancellation for Wednesday afternoon at three-thirty. Would that suit you?'

'Wednesday at three-thirty,' she repeated, glancing at Rick. He shrugged and nodded. 'That's perfect! Thank you so much, Lynne. I really appreciate it.'

She rang off and stowed her phone back into her bag. 'Three-thirty Wednesday,' she repeated.

'So you're intent on holding my hand?'

An edge had crept into his voice. She sat a little straighter and lifted her chin. 'It'll speed things up.'

'Why are you so intent on helping me get to the bottom of all this?'

She reached out to clasp the stem of her wine glass, twirled it around and around on the table. She lifted a shoulder. 'There are a few different reasons. Guilt, for one. Your father has been dead for eight months and I've only found the time to give you his letter now.'

'If he was my father.'

If.

'You had no idea what that letter contained. If you did…'

'I'd have tried to deliver it the same day! And I'd have quizzed John to within an inch of his life, but that's beside the point. I should've found the time to deliver it to you sooner.'

'You've had a lot on your plate these last eight months. You've no need to feel guilty.'

'The locket,' she whispered. 'It caused you so much trouble.'

'We were just kids, Nell. None of it was your fault.'

That wasn't true. 'I still feel badly about it.'

He reached out and for a moment she thought he meant to take her hand; at the last moment he pulled his hand back. 'I wish you wouldn't.'

He hadn't touched her but warmth threaded through his eyes. His mouth had lost its hard edge, replaced with a gentle sensuality that threatened to weave her under its spell. She knew in her bones that Rick would know how to kiss a woman and mean it.

It took all her strength to suppress the thrill that rippled through her. She fumbled to find the thread of their conversation again. 'The police labelled you a thief and a liar,' she forced herself to say. 'They thought you bullied me into handing the locket over. Those labels stuck.'

'Not my fault, Nell. And not yours.'

Because he seemed to want her to, she nodded. 'Anything else?'

'John,' she sighed. 'I can't help feeling he'd want me to help you and...I don't owe him, but he was kind to me.'

He shot back in his chair, his eyes cold.

Her heart thumped. 'I'm not trying to justify his behaviour to you. That's shocking and unforgivable.' But Rick would never have found the marigold tin without her help and what if there was further nonsense to be endured during the solicitor's appointment?

All of the hard angles had shot back into Rick's face. A lazy devil's smile hovered about his mouth, but it didn't reach his eyes. She pulled herself up, lifted her chin and gave the most speaking shrug in her armoury. 'Of course, if you'd prefer I didn't attend the appointment on Wednesday, obviously I won't.' She reached for her glass and took a sip, pretending it was something French and priceless.

Just like that, Rick laughed and the devil leached out of him. 'What a pair we are.'

'What are you talking about?'

He dismissed that with a flick of his fingers. 'If you think it'll make the meeting more profitable then I'd appreciate your presence.'

She took another sip, glad this time that it was just plain old Chardonnay. 'Okay.'

'What's more, I'll thank you in advance and mean it. Thank you, Nell.'

'You're welcome.'

'This, however—' he lifted his glass and drained the last mouthful '—is awful.'

She feigned outrage, but he only grinned. 'I know where Garside's office is. It's on the high street, right?' She nodded. 'Would you like to grab a coffee beforehand?'

'Oh.' Her face fell. 'That's a really nice idea, Rick, but—'

'You have other plans. No sweat.' He rose as if

it were of no consequence. She wished it felt that way to her. Coffee invitations had been few and far between these last few months. 'I'll see you out the front at three-twenty-five.'

She rose too. 'Right.'

'Correct me if I'm wrong, Nell… You don't mind if I call you Nell, do you?'

Nell suppressed a shudder at the wet smile Clint Garside turned on her. 'Not at all.'

'I was under the impression that the business you wished to discuss concerned yourself.'

She forced her eyes wide. 'Oh, but it does, Mr Garside. It's just before we get to that I was hoping we'd be able to clear up this little matter for Mr Bradford and my family's former employee, the late Mr John Cox. It's been such a weight on my mind.'

'Well…of course, of course.'

He smoothed his hair back and sent her another greasy smile. He barely glanced at Rick. She'd forgive him the smarminess, but she wouldn't forgive him for ignoring Rick. He had no right to his snobbery. He had no right thinking he was better than Rick.

'You have to understand, however, that it may take my staff and I some time to locate the file. It's an older case and I'm sure you appreciate—'

'Oh, I do hope not.' Nell crossed her leg and smoothed a hand down the bodice of her dress. 'Once that document is found I was hoping to discuss the possibility of selling Whittaker House with you. I wanted to know if you'd be interested in handling the conveyancing of the property for me?'

She traced fingers along the V-neck of her dress, drawing the solicitor's eyes there, and she could've sworn that beside her Rick was trying not to laugh. She didn't dare glance at him for fear that a fit of giggles might overtake her.

She tossed her hair back and assumed the most superior posture she could. 'Of course, I couldn't possibly consider that while I have loose ends like this one hanging over my head.' She sighed and made to rise. 'Perhaps you'll be so kind as to call me once you've found the relevant documentation and then we can take it from there.'

'Oh, please sit, Nell. Let's not be too hasty.' Clint Garside rushed around the desk and urged Nell back into her seat. 'Let me just have a quick look to see if they're near at hand after all.'

'Why, of course.' She beamed at him. 'I can't tell you how much I appreciate all the trouble you're taking.'

Rick snorted. Clint glanced at him sharply and Nell reached out to touch the solicitor's arm and recapture his attention before elbowing Rick in the ribs. 'The file?' she reminded him gently.

'Oh, yes.' He was all smarmy smiles again. He patted her hand before trotting over to a filing cabinet on the other side of the room. *Ugh!* Behind his back, she wiped her hand down her skirt. The man had a touch like a dead fish.

'Bingo!' Clint turned with another wide, wet smile and held a file aloft. And for no reason at all her heart started to hammer. Was this the moment Rick would discover the identity of his sibling?

'So…' Clint sat across from her at his desk again, the file closed in front of him '…about Whittaker House…'

Beside her, she could feel Rick bunch up with tension. 'Yes, it's such a responsibility owning a house like that, but…' She gave a delicate little cough and glanced sideways to indicate Rick. 'Perhaps we can take care of this matter first and then…talk in private?'

His eyes gleamed. 'Why yes, of course.'

He opened the file and glanced at what she supposed must be John's instructions. 'There's nothing too difficult here. The late Mr Cox left a letter for Mr Rick Bradford should Mr Bradford ever come to collect it. The letter will need to be signed for, of course.'

'Of course,' she echoed.

'But, before that can happen, Mr Bradford has to provide a password.'

The air left her in a rush. Her entire body slumped like a deflated balloon before she had the foresight to shake herself upright again. She turned to Rick, trying to swallow her panic. *A password?*

'You will only get one chance, Mr Bradford.'

Acid burned her throat. 'Oh, Rick…'

He merely grinned at her, those dark eyes dancing. 'Don't sweat it, Princess.' He turned to the solicitor. 'The password will be Marigold.'

'That's correct.'

Marigold? He was a genius!

'All you now need to do is sign here.' Clint handed Rick a pen without looking at him and indicated where he should sign. His lack of courtesy grated on her. Hadn't the people around here heard that Rick's name had been cleared?

Ah, but there's no smoke without fire. Her lip curled at the narrow-minded pettiness of it all.

Rick read the short statement, signed and took the letter from Clint's outstretched hand. He clasped her shoulder briefly. 'Thanks, Nell.'

And then he left. She wondered if she'd ever see him again.

Seven and three-quarter minutes later Nell made her escape from Clint Garside. With what she hoped was a breezy wave to Lynne, she shot outside to drag a breath of air into lungs that had cramped.

'Hey, Princess.'

She spun around to find Rick leaning against the wall just outside the door. One leg slightly raised, knee bent so his foot rested on the wall behind too. The epitome of casual indolence and she had to swallow to contain the leap of joy her heart gave at seeing him.

Slowly, she eased a breath of air out of lungs that had cramped up in an entirely different way. Rick wore a pair of dark denim jeans and a white business shirt, top button undone—no tie—and with the sleeves rolled up to his forearms. He looked like a model for a jeans commercial.

'Everything okay?'

She should be the one asking that. She swallowed and nodded and tried not to swoon in relief that he'd waited. 'I wasn't sure if you'd still be here.'

'Why not?'

That intent dark gaze watched her as if…as if she were worth watching, she realised. As if he liked not just what he saw, but…her. As if he liked *her*.

No doubt it was all just a trick of the light. And if it wasn't it'd just be smoke and mirrors. Rick had a reputation where women were concerned. Flirting would be as natural as breathing to him.

'I thought you might like to be alone to read John's letter.'

He glanced away and she took a step closer. 'What did it say?'

One of those broad shoulders lifted. 'I haven't opened it yet.'

She stared at those shoulders and bit her lip. A hum started up in her blood. She stretched out her toes to prevent them from curling.

'The street didn't seem like the right place. I'd prefer more privacy than that.'

Did he want to go home? Or maybe he wanted privacy, but didn't want to be totally alone? 'You could come back to Whittaker House with me if you like.'

One corner of his mouth hitched up. It made her blood chug. 'You're dying of curiosity, aren't you?'

'Absolutely,' she agreed. 'But there are cupcakes at my place. There's a Salted Caramel with my name on it.'

'Is there one for me?'

She gave an exaggerated roll of her eyes. 'Of course there is. I would never be so cruel as to eat one in front of company without offering them around first. You can have the Cherry Cheesecake and the Bubblegum if you like.'

'Sold!' He pushed away from the wall and fell into step beside her. 'Did you drive?'

She shook her head. 'It's only a five-minute walk—did you?'

'Nah, it's only about two minutes from Tash's.'

They walked along in silence. She was aware of the heat and magnetism he gave off, of the grace with which his tall body moved and the confidence in his strides—shortened to match hers at the moment. With each step she took, her awareness of him grew.

'You were magnificent back there, you know?'

'Me? You were the one who guessed the password!'

'You had that slimy solicitor eating out of the palm of your hand.'

She snorted. 'That was nothing more than him being overtaken by his own greed.'

'You played him to perfection. I went into that meeting determined to stamp my mark on it, but...'

She pushed a strand of hair behind her ear and dared to meet his gaze. 'But?'

'You were an absolute delight to watch and I didn't want to interrupt you. I can't remember the last time I enjoyed myself so much.'

Her cheeks warmed. 'I was pretty good, wasn't I?' she said because she didn't want him to see how much his words touched her.

He threw his head back and laughed. 'Did you crush him like a bug when I left?'

'I was tempted to, but no.'

He eased back to survey her. 'Why not?'

She kept her gaze straight ahead. 'It doesn't do to make enemies.' She had enough of those as it was. 'He thinks I'm exploring my options and that he's number one on my go-to list. Besides, I didn't want to burn our bridges where he was concerned until after you'd read your letter.' Who knew when they might have to consult with him again?

He didn't say anything so she forced herself to smile up at him. 'I'll save squashing him for another day.'

Her heart started to thump. Hard. She had to tread carefully—very carefully. She was in danger of turning this man into her Sir Galahad. Just as she'd done as a ten-year-old...and throughout her early teens—the fantasy boy who'd ride up on his white charger and rescue her.

She scowled and picked up her pace. Well, she was no damsel. And Rick Bradford wasn't a Sir Galahad in anybody's language.

CHAPTER FOUR

NELL BUSTLED ABOUT the kitchen, putting the coffee on to percolate, arranging some of those sugary confections with their over-the-top frosting and decorations onto a plate and setting it on the table.

While Rick was aware of Nell's activity, all he could focus on was the letter he'd placed on the table. Sun poured in through the windows over the sink and a warm breeze wafted through the wide open back door and the kitchen gleamed in spotless—if somewhat crowded—cleanliness. And yet none of it could hold his attention.

The envelope sat on the table and the black capitals seemed to sneer at him. He deliberately turned to Nell. 'When did you move back in here, Princess?'

'Friday.'

His head snapped back. 'Friday? As in five days ago?'

'That's right.' She poured out two mugs of steaming coffee. She wore another frock. This one was

white with cherries printed all over it and she had a
red patent leather belt cinched at her waist.

She'd moved in on Friday, met all of her weekend orders, had dealt with the suit *and* had found
the time to help him out too? And she hadn't com-
plained. Not once. She hadn't made him feel as if
he were in the way or as if she had more important
things to do.

Why?

Because of a silly incident fifteen years ago and a
sense of responsibility to a dead man? He dropped
into a chair, his chest heavy.

She sat too. She glanced at the letter, but she didn't
ask about it. Instead, she selected a cupcake and cut
it into quarters, sliced one quarter in half and with
the crumb delicately held between thumb and forefinger she brought it to her mouth. Her lips closed
about it and she let out a breath, her eyes half closing.

He swallowed. If the taste and texture of salted
caramel did that to her, he wondered what she'd look
like if she licked whipped cream from his—

He shot back in his chair, hot and hard. Hell!
Where had *that* come from? Gritting his teeth, he
tried to shake his mind free from the scent of sugar.
He gulped coffee instead and scalded his tongue.

'Ignoring it won't make it go away.' She broke off
another crumb. He averted his gaze as she lifted it
towards her mouth. She was silent for a moment.

'You really aren't sure yet if you do want a brother or a sister, are you?'

He'd already told her that. 'You don't get it?' Why he'd expected her to understand he couldn't begin to explain. They might've grown up in the same neighbourhood, but they came from completely different worlds.

'I think I do. You're afraid this unknown sibling will reject you.'

Her candour sliced into the heart of him. He held himself tight so he couldn't flinch.

'I'd be afraid of that too.'

The simple admission eased some of the previous sting. 'Who in their right mind would reject you, Princess?'

'I know. It's inconceivable, isn't it?' She lifted her nose in the air and gave an elegant shrug, but it was so over the top he found himself biting back a grin.

He let a part of the grin free and reached for a cake.

'You're afraid your history—having been to jail and whatnot—will mean they won't want anything to do with you.'

He bit into the cupcake, barely tasting it.

'And yet you're also afraid your sibling could be on the same path you were, that he or she may need help.'

It took all of his strength to swallow without choking. Acid churned in his stomach.

'There's no easy answer to any of that, is there?'

He couldn't bear to look at her. He wasn't sure he could stand the sympathy he suspected he would find in her face. He pushed his chair back and sat side on to the table.

'You do know you don't have to address those concerns yet, though, don't you?'

Very slowly, he turned back to her. Her face wasn't full of sympathy, but rather no-nonsense practicality.

'You can find out who this sibling is and then make the decision about whether to approach them or not.'

She had a point. In fact she made a very good point. He straightened. If all was well and good in his sibling's life, he could walk away without a pang.

Liar.

If all weren't well, maybe he'd find a way to help them anonymously.

Or maybe he'd introduce himself. Maybe he'd give family another shot and—

He clenched his eyes and closed his mind to that possibility. It was too soon to think about it, too soon to get caught up in the fairy tale Nell harboured— that this would end well for everyone. This was the real world and, more often than not, in the real world things didn't work out.

That didn't change the fact that on this point she was right—he didn't need to make every decision at this current moment in time. He went to reach for the envelope when she said, 'It's also occurred to me...'

She bit her lip. It made her look incredibly young. He pulled his hand back. 'What?'

She grimaced. 'What if John left a letter for your sibling with sleazy solicitor Garside—to be opened at some future date?'

He stiffened.

'What if at some time in the future this sibling turns up on your doorstep? Wouldn't it be better to...' She trailed off as if she didn't know how to finish that sentence despite all of her surface polish.

His hand clenched to a fist. 'You're saying fore-warned is forearmed?'

They stared at each other for a moment. Eventually she shook her head. 'I don't know what I'm saying.'

Her chin lifted. 'Yes, I do. I'm saying read the darn letter, Rick, and then maybe you'll enjoy your cupcake.'

It surprised a laugh out of him. The Princess had changed from the shy little kid and the awkward teenager. He wanted to ask her about the transformation, only he suspected she'd chide him for changing the subject and avoiding the obvious.

And she'd probably be right.

He tore open the letter. He tried not to think too hard about what he was doing. It didn't stop the skin of his scalp tightening over until it became one big prickling itch.

The envelope contained a single sheet of folded paper. His hand trembled—just for a fraction of a second—and that sign of weakness make him want to smash something. He glanced at Nell to see if she'd noticed, but she was intent on reducing her cupcake to a pile of crumbs. He let out a breath and unfolded the sheet of paper.

He stared and stared.

And then he let loose with the rudest word he knew.

Nell jumped. Her chin shot up. 'I beg your pardon?'

'Sorry,' he growled. Not that he felt the least bit remorseful.

She moistened her bottom lip and he was suddenly and ravenously hungry. For a moment it seemed that if he could lose himself in her for an hour he'd find the answer to ease the burn in his soul.

As if she'd read that thought in his eyes, she drew back, but pink stained her cheeks and her breathing had grown shallower. If he wanted, he could seduce her. Right here, right now.

If he wanted...

A harsh laugh broke from him. Oh, he wanted all right, but there was always a price to pay for seducing a woman. The price for this woman would be too high.

He leapt out of his chair and wheeled away, his hands clenched to fists.

'Please don't punch a wall. I already have enough holes to mend.'

Her words couldn't drag even a ghost of a smile from him.

'I take it, then, that you recognise the name John has given you?'

Name? *Ha!* He wheeled back and thrust the letter at her. With a wary glance up at him she took it. She stared at him for two beats more, looked as if she wanted to say something, and then with the tiniest of shrugs turned her gaze to the letter.

She frowned. She turned it over and then back. She held it up to the light. The frown deepened to a scowl. She slammed it down to the table. 'But this doesn't make sense!'

'It's obviously some kind of code.'

'A code?'

She swore then too and it surprised him so much his head rocked back.

'Of all the mean-spirited pieces of spite!' She leapt up, hands clenched and eyes narrowed, as she paced up and down beside the table. 'Not only does he spend your *entire* childhood ignoring you—' she flung an arm out '—but now he plagues you with nonsense and taunts you with a carrot he keeps whisking out of reach.'

She ended on an incoherent growl of frustration. Rick eased back to lean against the wall. The Princess wasn't just cross—she was hopping mad. In fact, she was a great big ball of boiling rage.

She stabbed a finger in his direction. 'If I could get hold of him now I'd make his ears burn, let me tell you.' She slammed a hand to the table. 'Well, we'll just crack that code! And to hell with him!'

She glanced at Rick, stilled and then rolled her shoulders. 'What?'

'Who are you really angry with, Princess?'

The colour leached from her face. 'I don't know what you're talking about.' She took her seat and crossed her legs, polished and smooth once more.

He sat too. Even though he knew he should leave.

She pushed the sheet of paper back across to him. 'All of these letters and numbers—they have to mean something.'

Did he really want to bother with any of this? He raked both hands through his hair and fought the exhaustion that washed over him. If he walked away now, what would be the worst-case scenario?

The answer came to him too swiftly. He reached for a cupcake, needing the sweetness to counter the bitterness that rose up through him. The worst-case scenario would be at some point in the future to come face to face with a younger version of himself—a kid he could've helped. A kid he'd chosen to reject in the same way John had rejected him. How could he justify walking away to that kid when he'd had the chance to discover the truth?

Could he live with that?

Maybe, but in his bones he knew he didn't want to.

Damn it all to hell!

He came back to himself to find Nell copying the code onto a notepad. 'What are you doing?'

'Making a copy.'

'Why?'

She'd taken this too personally—as if John had lied to her.

'I'm going to do an Internet search on codes tonight to see what I can find out.'

'Nell, this isn't your problem.'

'That's not what it feels like.' She finished and pushed the letter back towards him. 'Besides, it won't hurt to have a copy.'

He supposed not.

'C'mon.' She rose. 'We haven't checked John's cottage yet. There might be a box or two of his belongings left behind, something that might give us a clue.'

He rose. What he should do was thank her for her help, and tell her this was no longer her problem. Except…it wouldn't hurt to check out where John Cox had spent over thirty years of his life. It might give him a sense of the man. He'd take anything to gain some leverage in this wild goose chase.

And then he could leave.

For good.

He couldn't prevent a sense of déjà vu when they stepped out of the back door and made their way across the terrace. The yellow heads of dandelions waved in the breeze. Nell pointed to one. 'I've always kind of liked them. They're cheery, don't you think? I must've spread a whole forest of them throughout the garden. I loved it when they turned puffy and I could blow their seed heads and set them free. I used to think if I could blow the entire seed head off in one breath and make a wish it'd come true.'

'Did your wishes ever come true?'

She lifted an eminently elegant shoulder. 'I expect one or two must've, I made so many. Law of averages would suggest so.'

She was lying. He wasn't sure how he knew. Maybe it was the way she lifted a hand to her face to brush an imaginary strand of hair back behind her ear. Maybe it was the way she studiously avoided meeting his gaze.

And maybe he was watching her just a little too closely? Gritting his teeth, he forced his eyes to the front.

They passed the garden shed. They moved beyond Nell's first flowerbed until they reached the very back of the property. Nell pushed open a gate in a six-foot-high bamboo fence to reveal a cottage on the other side. Rick followed. 'You'd have no idea this was here if you didn't know about it.'

'That's the point. Heaven forbid that one should catch a glimpse of where the hired help live.'

He couldn't tell from either her voice or her bearing whether she subscribed to that view or not. She didn't give him the time to figure it out either, but strode up the two steps leading to the cottage's ve-

randa and reached for the door handle…and then
came up short when it didn't budge. She turned back
to him with a shrug. 'Locked. I wonder where the
set of master keys for the property can be?'

He knew how to pick a lock…

Nell moved back down the steps, dropped to her
knees and reached beneath the veranda. When she
drew her hand back she held a key.

It hit him then that he wouldn't be able to just
walk away. Nell knew his father and this property
like no one else did. If he wanted to solve this mystery he was going to need her help.

Nell was going to be the key.

Nell tossed the key to Rick.

He caught it as if he'd been catching curve balls
all of his life. Which was probably true. She bit back
a sigh. She couldn't change Rick's past any more
than she could change her own.

'You can do the honours,' she told him.

'Why?'

She blinked. 'What on earth do you mean—why?'
She didn't feel like explaining her ambivalence. 'Because you're closer.'

'Was closer,' he corrected.

How was it possible for this man to divine her
private moods so accurately? *Who are you really
angry with?* She shied away from that one. 'As far as
I know, this place hasn't been disturbed in months.

If there're any creepy-crawlies in there you can en-counter them first.'

'I'm not buying that for a moment, Princess. I just saw the way you stuck your hand beneath the ve-randa. You're not afraid of spiders or insects.'

'What about ghosts?' The words shot out of her before she could pull them back. She grimaced at his raised eyebrow. 'Not a literal one. Ghosts from the past.'

She ruffled out the skirt of her dress to give her an excuse not to look at him. 'This area was always out of bounds to me when I was a child. I'm still not feeling a hundred per cent easy being here.'

'Princess, you own this cottage. It's yours. You have every right to be here.'

She lifted her chin and considered him. He raised that eyebrow then, as if daring her. She plucked the key from his fingers, stuck it in the lock and turned it. 'I don't even know if the power's still connected.' She swung the door open, but when she tried the switch, light flooded the room.

She stepped inside with Rick at her heels. The door led straight into the living room. 'I've never been in here before,' she murmured, 'so I don't know the layout.'

This room and the adjoining kitchen were sparsely furnished but, other than a faint layer of dust, it was remarkably clean and tidy. She strode across to the kitchen area and hunted through the cupboards. 'There's some crockery, cooking utensils and cutlery, but there doesn't seem to be anything personal,' she said, turning back to the living area.

'Not much in here either,' Rick said, closing the drawer of the sideboard.

'Maybe we'll have more luck in the bedrooms.'

But, other than a bed, a mattress encased in plastic—presumably to protect it from the dust—and some linens, they found no trace of John Cox's presence in either of the two bedrooms. It was as if he'd been washed away when the cleaners had come in. Whoever her father had hired, they'd done their job to perfection.

Nell dropped to the wooden chair that sat at the desk in the smaller of the two bedrooms. Had John used this room as a study? If so, what had he studied? What, other than gardening, had he been interested in?

Other than avoiding his paternal duties, that was.

She glanced at Rick. She couldn't tell what impression the cottage had made on him. If any.

He turned as if he'd felt the weight of her gaze. 'You were hoping we'd find something.'

'Of course I was. Weren't you?'

'I thought it a fool's mission from the beginning.'

Oh, great. She glared at the ceiling. So not only was she a spoiled little rich girl, but she was a fool too? She straightened when she realised what she was staring at. 'A loft hatch.' She rose and set her chair beneath it and then gestured for Rick to investigate further.

'If there's anything at all up there, Princess, it'll only be porn magazines.'

'Look, I'm not tall enough to reach it properly so just humour me, okay?'

He didn't move. He just stared at her instead. She lifted her arms and let them drop. 'If I have to go and get the ladder from the shed to do it myself I will.'

With a smothered something she was glad she didn't catch, Rick hauled himself up on the chair and pushed the loft cover to one side. Pulling himself up, he peered inside.

Nell surveyed the way his forearm muscles bunched and the promise of bulging biceps. Not to mention the long clean line of his back. Her heart pitter-pattered. Her fingers curled into her palms, even as her tongue touched the corner of her mouth.

Rick had been a good-looking youth, but it was nothing to the man he'd become. And in those jeans there was no denying that he was all man.

And the stupid fluttering in her throat reminded her that she wasn't the kind of woman who was immune to Rick's particular brand of masculinity. Not that she had any intention of doing anything more than looking.

'There's something up here.'

That snapped her to. 'What is it?'

If only it'd give them another piece of the puzzle. Or, barring that, a clue as to how to solve that stupid coded message.

'I'm going up.'

With that, he disappeared completely into the ceiling space. Nell paced down below. 'What is it?' she called up again.

'Some kind of box.'

'Are there any photos in it? A family tree or birth certificates or—'

His face appeared at the hole and he laughed down at her. 'You really are the eternal optimist, aren't you?'

Her face fell.

'It's locked,' he said. 'Here—I'll pass it down to you.'

She had to stand on the chair to reach it. When she was on the ground again, he swung himself back down beside her. 'Don't worry, Princess. I'm a dab hand at picking a lock.'

She couldn't drag her gaze from the box.

'Nell?'

She swallowed and forced her gaze up to his. 'We won't need to pick the lock.' She handed him the box and reached up to open the locket at her throat. She removed the tiny key it contained.

His gaze narrowed. 'Where did you get that?'

She touched the locket. 'This was my grandmother's. And that—' she nodded at the box '—is her jewellery box.'

He stared at her and the lines around his mouth turned white. 'John Cox stole your grandmother's jewels?'

She laughed. It held little mirth, though it was

better than sitting in the middle of the room and bawling her eyes out. 'I don't think he stole them. I think he probably saved them.'

Comprehension dawned in his eyes. 'From your father?'

'From my father.' Before she'd died, her grandmother had owned a couple of nice pieces. Nell had thought them long gone.

He slung an arm about her shoulders and led her back into the living room. He placed the box on the tiny kitchen table and pushed her into one of the two chairs. He sat in the other. Even though he'd removed his arm she could still feel the warm weight of it and the lean coiled power of his body as he'd walked beside her. He smelt like dust and something smoky and aromatic like paprika.

'Aren't you going to open it?'

Of course she was. It was just…she'd never expected to see this box again. She missed her grandmother. Seeing this only made her miss her more.

His face darkened. 'Or would you prefer to take it back to the big house and open it in private?'

Her spine stiffened. Her chin lifted. 'I never once thought you a thief, Rick Bradford!' A temptation, definitely, and one she fully intended to resist, but a thief? No.

For a moment his slouch lost some of its insolence. 'Goes to show what you know, Nell Smythe-Whittaker. My teenage shoplifting is on police record.'

'I'm not even going to dignify that with an answer.' She pulled the box towards her, unlocked it and lifted the lid. Her breath caught. 'Oh, her rings! I remember her wearing these.' She had to swallow a lump. 'My grandfather gave her this one.' She touched a large diamond ring. 'And this emerald belonged to her grandmother. The gold signet belonged to her mother.' She lifted them out one by one and passed them to Rick.

'The diamond and the emerald might fetch you a bit.'

'I couldn't sell them!'

She knew he wouldn't understand her sentimentality, but…her grandmother was the only person in her life who'd loved her unconditionally.

'How old were you when she died?'

'Seventeen.'

'That must've been tough.'

Sure, but it was nothing compared to all Rick had been through in his life. 'Oh, look.' She lifted a shoulder in a wry shrug. 'John has left me a letter.'

He rolled his eyes. 'He's turning out to be the regular correspondent.'

Dear Miss Nell,
If you've found your grandma's box then I expect you know why I hid it. I'm sorry I couldn't rescue it all before your daddy got a hold of the diamond necklace.

She stopped to glance into the box. 'Yep, gone,' she clarified.

'We only have John's word it was your father who took it.'

'And my knowledge of my father.'

Rick straightened. Unfortunately, it didn't make his shoulders any the less droolworthy. 'Hell, Nell.'

'Hell's bells, Nell, has an even better ring to it,' she told him, resisting the sympathy in his eyes and choosing flippancy instead.

Who are you really angry with?

She cleared her throat and smoothed out the sheet of paper.

I know the old lady meant these for you, and I know you'd want to pass them on to your own daughters when the time comes.
Regards, John.

She folded the letter and put it back in the box. Silently, Rick put the rings back on top. Nell locked it. She pulled in a breath and then met his gaze. 'Rick, would you please put this back where you found it?'

His head rocked back. 'Why? You should at least wear this stuff if you're not going to sell it. You should at least enjoy remembering your grandmother.'

In an ideal world...

She moistened her lips. 'The set of master keys for Whittaker House are nowhere to be found. Until

I find them I can't…' She halted, swallowed. 'What I'm trying to say is that I can't think of a safer place to keep them than where we found them.'

'You're forgetting one thing.'

'What's that?'

'*I* know where they are.'

'I've already told you that I don't believe you're a thief.'

'No, but I do mean to make you a proposal, Princess, and that might change how you feel about things.'

CHAPTER FIVE

NELL'S HEART STUTTERED at the casual way Rick uttered the word *proposal*. It held such promise and she knew that promise was a lie.

Oh, not a lie on his behalf, but on hers. She wanted to invest it with more meaning than he could ever hope to give it—a carry-over from her childhood fantasies of making things right over the locket.

The childhood fantasy of having one true friend.

But Rick didn't know any of that. The man in front of her might look like the boy who'd starred in her fantasies, but inside she didn't doubt that her boy and the real Rick were very different people.

Life hadn't been kind to Rick Bradford.

And she needed to remember he had no reason to think kindly or act kindly towards her.

He stared at her with those dark eyes and she drew a long breath into her lungs. 'Proposal?' She was proud her voice didn't tremble.

'I was going to leave Sydney at the end of the week.'

That didn't give them much time to crack John's code.

'I've holidayed long enough and it's time to be doing something.'

She couldn't help herself. 'What do you do for work?' Did he have a regular job?

'I usually pick up some building labourer's work here and there.'

So, that'd be a no then.

He grinned—a lazy insolent thing, as if he'd read her mind. 'I don't like being tied down to one thing for too long.'

She knew then he was talking about women and relationships too.

'I like my freedom.'

Given how his freedom had been curtailed in prison, she could understand that.

A prison sentence he should never have had to serve, though. A prison sentence he had served because a woman had taken advantage of him.

'What are you thinking about?' he suddenly barked and she jumped.

'How awful jail must've been.' It didn't occur to her to lie, but when his face turned grey she wished she had. 'I'm sorry you were sent to jail for something you didn't do, Rick.'

'It's all in the past.'

The words came out icily from between uncompromising lips and Nell had to suppress a shiver. He'd carry the scars of jail with him forever. She glanced down at her hands before lifting her chin. She had no right picking the scabs off those wounds. 'You said you *were* planning to leave Sydney, as in past tense. Have you changed your mind?'

His eyes blazed. He stabbed a finger to the table and dust rose up in the air around him. His crisp white shirt, his hands and hair all sported streaks of dust and cobwebs. She guessed the skirt of her dress wasn't in much better shape. It was the kind of carelessness that as a child had earned her rebuke after rebuke from her mother.

She forced her chin up higher. Well, her mother was off somewhere with husband number four and Nell was old enough to do what she darn well pleased. She didn't have to answer to anyone.

But those dirty streaks on Rick's shirt reminded her that while he'd been convicted of a crime he hadn't committed, it didn't necessarily make him a law-abiding citizen. It didn't mean he wasn't a heart-breaker who'd take advantage of weakness when he saw it in others.

And you're weak.

She swallowed. Correction. She had been weak. Past tense.

He continued to glare at her with those blazing eyes but he didn't say anything. She made her voice as impersonal as she could. 'You were saying?'

He pushed away from the table and paced to the other side of the room before striding back. 'I'm going to get to the bottom of this bloody mystery!'

He spat out his *bloody* with so much anger she couldn't help wincing.

He dragged a hand down his face, glancing back at her with hooded eyes. 'Sorry.'

She shook her head, cursing her own prissiness. 'You don't have to apologise. I understand your venom.'

'You know what, Princess?' He took his seat again. 'I believe you do.'

She didn't want to follow that conversational thread so she merely said, 'I think it wise to try and discover who your sibling might be.'

'Except I've overstayed my welcome at Tash's.'

She doubted that.

'Besides, she's in love. I'm cramping her style.' He grimaced. 'And I can't stomach much more of her and Mitch's lovey-dovey stuff.'

That sounded more like it.

For some reason, the skin on her arms started to chill.

'So what I was going to suggest is that you let me use this cottage rent-free for the next few weeks. I mean, it's just sitting here doing nothing.'

The chill spread up her neck and down her spine.

'And in return I'll do some work on the big house.'

The chill disappeared. He didn't mean to take advantage of her after all?

'What kind of work?'

He lifted one lazy shoulder. 'Whatever repairs I manage to get to and maybe even some painting.'

That would be brilliant! She opened her mouth to snap up his offer before he could retract it, but a glance in his direction had her closing it again. Rick had a look in his eyes that she recognised. A look she'd seen in her father's eyes—an *I'm going to get my own way and I don't care by what methods* look.

She wasn't a pushover any more. Her father had discovered that and now Rick could too. She pushed her grandmother's jewellery box towards him. 'Put that back where we found it.'

'Is that a yes or a no to my proposal?'

'It's negotiations are underway but, regardless of the outcome, it doesn't affect the fate of the jewellery box.'

He leaned back and folded his arms. For a moment she thought he was going to refuse. And then she started. 'Heavens, where are my manners? Would you *please* put the box back in the ceiling?'

One side of his mouth hooked up. 'I wasn't waiting for a please, Princess.'

'I know, but there's no excuse for bad manners. Have you seen enough of the cottage to satisfy your purposes?'

'Yes.'

'Then I propose we go back up to the house and see if we can come to some arrangement that will satisfy mine.'

He laughed at that. She wished he hadn't. He looked younger, nicer, when he laughed and it had the potential to turn her to jelly.

She didn't need jelly but steel.

Without another word, Rick rose and placed the box back in the ceiling. Nell locked the door behind them and pocketed the key. Rick watched her, but he didn't say anything. In fact, neither one of them spoke on the walk back to the house.

When they reached it, Nell cleared her throat. 'I'd prefer to nail you down to specifics, Rick. How long do you think you'll stay?'

He shrugged. 'Can we start with a month?'

'Absolutely.' She pulled her no-nonsense business voice out and dusted it off. 'We can agree to a week-by-week arrangement if need be after that.'

'Fine.'

Was he laughing at her? She glanced across but couldn't tell. 'So, included in your four weeks' worth of repairs…' she walked through to the front of the house to the grand hall with its staircase that curved up to the first floor and pointed to the front door '…can you fix that?'

'Check.'

She didn't care if he was laughing at her. She tossed her head and walked into the grand parlour with its enormous bay window. 'Can you fix the hole in the wall?'

He walked over to it, tested it with his fingers, bent over to examine it more closely and the denim of his jeans stretched across those powerful thighs and taut butt and Nell had to swallow as her saliva glands kicked into overdrive. *Oh, my word.* Rick

Bradford filled out a pair of jeans to perfection. Her fingers fluttered about her throat. Her eyes widened in an effort to take in as much of the view as they could. A hunger, deep and gnawing, that no number of cupcakes would assuage, racked her.

Rick turned. 'This doesn't—'

He broke off, a grin bold and sure spreading across his face. Folding his arms, he leant a shoulder against the wall. 'See anything you like, Princess?'

Heat scalded her face. She wished the floor would open up and swallow her. 'Don't be ridiculous.' But her voice came out at a squeak, which only made his grin widen.

She gestured to the wall. 'You were saying?'

Very slowly, he sobered and straightened. 'I'm not on offer, Nell. I'm not part of the bargain.'

'I never for one moment considered you were.' How could he cheapen not only her but himself like that? And then she remembered his mother had been a prostitute.

She closed her eyes and swallowed. If she hadn't been weak fifteen years ago, if she'd stood up for Rick, she could walk away from all of this now and...

Oh, who was she kidding? It didn't erase her sense of responsibility towards John. The way he'd treated Rick was beyond the pale, but there had to be a reason for all of this—something they couldn't see yet.

She forced her eyes open. 'Can we please get back to the task at hand?'

His lips twisted. 'Gladly.' He gestured to the wall. 'This looks like damage caused by something hard or heavy being banged against it.'

That'd be the removal men her father had hired to pillage the house of its expensive antiques.

'I can replaster it and then paint the entire room.'

That was even worth putting up with Rick's mockery!

'Then you have yourself a deal.'

He laughed. 'You have no idea, do you?'

'What are you talking about?'

'So far we've nailed down about a week's worth of work.'

Was that all?

'I'll fix the guttering that's falling off the outside of the house—that's another day's work.'

Wow. Um... 'What about painting the outside of the house?' It was badly in need of it.

He shook his head. 'That's too big a job for one person. Given the style and heritage of this place, it'd be best left to the professionals. Besides, I'm not sure you could afford the materials at the moment if money is tight.'

Her mouth dried. 'How much would it cost?'

'For paint, scaffolding and labour? I wouldn't expect you to see any change from twenty grand.'

So much? She needed to sit down. Only there wasn't a stick of furniture in the room. And yet if she were to put her plan into action it would need to be done.

'I can ring around and get some quotes for you if you like?'

She nodded. 'I'll need it for the business plan I mean to take to the bank.'

'I know this is none of my business...'

She glanced up at him.

'But is this place really worth going into so much debt for?'

'Yes.' She'd made a promise—a promise she had no intention of breaking. Her hands clenched. She could make this work!

Rick walked across to her with that indolent loose-hipped stride that could make her mouth dry in a millisecond. He stopped less than two feet away. His hands went to his hips—lean, sexy hips—and he leaned in towards her with narrowed eyes. 'What are your plans for this place?'

A husband and babies—a family. Lots of laughter. And love. But until then...

'I'm going to turn Whittaker House into the most in-demand venue for high tea parties that Sydney has ever seen.'

He blinked. She waited for him to laugh and tell her she was crazy. Instead, he turned back to survey the room. 'That's a nice idea for an old place like this. What rooms are you planning to use as public rooms?'

'These two front reception rooms—the parlour and the drawing room—the dining room as it opens onto the terrace, and the library. They're all large rooms. For more intimate gatherings, there's the morning room and the conservatory.'

She took him through each of the rooms. They ended the tour in the dining room—a grand room with French windows that led out to the terrace. Rick walked around the room's perimeter, checking skirting boards, picture rails and the windows and doors. 'Everything looks in pretty good nick, just the odd minor repair here and there—nothing that some putty and a screwdriver wouldn't fix.'

She let out a breath.

'It could do with some freshening up, though.' He pursed his lips. 'I could paint the two front rooms and this dining room in a month.'

Her heart didn't leap with the same unadulterated joy as it had earlier.

He shuffled his feet. 'Actually, throw the library in too—there's not much to do in there.'

She bit her lip. 'How much will the materials cost?'

'Depends on the kind of paint you want. You'll need something durable. What colours were you after?'

'The Victorians weren't afraid of colour and these rooms are big enough to bring it off. I thought a peacock-blue and a jade-green for the two front rooms, maybe coral in here. The library is lined with bookcases and there's not a whole lot of wall to paint so maybe just a cream to prevent it from becoming too dark in there.'

How much would it all cost, though?

'This room opens onto the terrace and lawn. You might want to consider making this the green room to fit in with the garden theme and have the coral room at the front.'

'Oh, that's a nice idea.' She pulled in another breath. 'But how much is this going to cost me?'

He tapped a finger against his jaw before straightening and naming a figure that made her wince. She nodded. 'Okay, I can manage that.' Just. 'Rick, it looks as if you have yourself a deal.'

He sent her a sly smile. 'Not so fast, Princess—negotiations aren't over yet.'

They weren't?

'You drive a hard bargain.'

He'd have had an easy one if he hadn't been so honest.

'In exchange for all of this slaving away on your house, I now have an additional demand.'

She folded her arms. 'Which is?'

Just for a moment his gaze lowered to her lips. Her breath stuttered. Oh, he couldn't mean…?

They both snapped away from each other at the same time.

'That you provide me with half a dozen cupcakes a day. A working man needs to keep up his strength.'

She planted her hands to her hips. 'Rick, you can't eat six cupcakes a day. You'll rot your teeth and make yourself sick.' She stuck out her jaw. 'How about two cupcakes a day and I'll throw in some sandwiches?'

'Four cupcakes and some sandwiches.'

Did he eat properly? Tash was probably taking care of that at the moment. How was he off for money? Not that she could talk, but she was making enough to cover the food bill and she still had some in her savings account, which would cover the cost of paint and materials. Sure, he might be getting rent-free accommodation, but he wouldn't be earning while he was here. She blew out a breath. 'And I'll throw in a Sunday roast.'

'Now you're talking.'

'C'mon.' She led him back into the kitchen. Taking a seat at the table, she dragged a notepad towards her and wrote out a brief contract outlining what they'd agreed to. She signed it and then pushed it across to him.

'You think this necessary?'

'I've learned not to take chances.'

His eyes darkened. 'You're prepared to trust me with your Gran's jewels, but not take my word about our deal?'

'I told you already—I don't believe you're a thief.' She glared because he made her feel self-conscious. 'It doesn't necessarily follow, though, that I trust you.'

Rick's heart burned for her, mourned that wide-eyed little girl who'd smiled at him with such open-heartedness it had made him believe there were better things in the world than he'd experienced up to that point.

'That sounds like hard-won wisdom, Princess.'

She didn't answer. He signed her contract because he wanted her to trust him. For good or ill.

'You've changed, Princess. A lot.'

She snorted. 'You mean I'm not fat any more?'

'Don't use that word!' His voice came out sharper than he intended, but he couldn't help it. Reverberating through his head, all he could hear were insults—*You're a fat piece of useless lard! How could anyone love you? You're fat and ugly!* Horrible things flung at women by men who'd meant to wound.

Nell eyed him warily. He glared at her. 'You were never fat!'

Her gaze slid sideways. She lifted a shoulder. 'I was plump, and I was awkward and almost chronically shy.'

Those things were true. 'I always thought you were kind of cute.'

That made her look back at him. She tried to hide it, but he could tell she wanted to believe him. 'If that's the case,' she said eventually, 'then you were in the minority.'

He still thought her cute, but he had no intention of acting on it. She was still trouble. And he avoided trouble wherever he could. And power games. And complications. He pushed his shoulders back. 'So how'd you go from shy and awkward to polished and sophisticated?'

She waved that away. 'It's too boring for words.'

Her reluctance intrigued him. 'I'd like to know.'

She blew out a breath before jumping up to put coffee on to percolate. He was about to tell her she drank too much caffeine but then she proceeded to set out some of her extraordinary cupcakes and he decided to keep his trap shut.

'Blueberry Delight and Tutti-Frutti,' she said, pointing. She made coffee and sat again.

He raised an eyebrow. 'Well?'

'As you've probably gathered, I wasn't precisely the kind of child my parents had been hoping for.' She blew on her coffee. 'They'd hoped for some pretty, delicate little thing who did ballet and uttered childish whimsies that charmed everyone.'

He winced. Nell hadn't fitted that picture.

'When I became a teenager, my mother hoped I'd become a fashion plate who'd be eager to accompany her on her many shopping expeditions.'

'And your father?'

'Who knows? He'd have probably been happy if his golf buddies made comments about me becoming a heartbreaker and that he'd have to beat the boys away with a big stick.'

Did she know that was exactly how she could be described now?

'When my grandmother found out how miserable I was she set about helping me.'

'How?'

'She took me to a therapist who helped me overcome my shyness. She took me to a stylist who trained me in what clothes and make-up best suited me, and she found me an up-and-coming young hairdresser who was an absolute whizz.' She sipped her coffee. 'Obviously, it didn't all happen overnight.'

Rick unclenched a hand to reach for a cupcake. 'You know your parents were wrong to have such expectations?' They should both be horsewhipped for making her feel like a failure, because she hadn't met their specific designer mould. People like that shouldn't have kids.

'I do now.'

He took a savage bite of cake and frosting. 'I mean, would you ever do that to a kid?'

Her eyes flashed. 'No!'

He set the cupcake back on his plate and eyed her for a long moment. 'Why all this determination to avoid self-pity?'

Something inside her eyes hardened. 'Because, regardless of my gripes about my parents, I never had it as tough as you or Tash or even Crazy Cheryl who you went to prison for.' She gave a half smile. 'Cheryl used to throw stones at me whenever she saw me in the garden.'

It didn't surprise him. Cheryl's home life had been beyond shocking. But…there was more than one way to damage a kid.

'It's not a contest, Princess.' She was entitled to her pain and disappointment.

'Tell that to my parents.'

Exhaustion hit him at the expression on her face. 'It didn't work, did it?' He slumped back. 'Did they notice at all?'

'They noticed. It just took me a long time to realise that it didn't make any difference, that it didn't make them love me more. It just meant they didn't mind parading me around their friends so much.'

He wanted to swear, but he knew she wouldn't like it so he didn't.

'And then I realised I was wasting all of this time going to parties I didn't enjoy, buying clothes I didn't want and doing coffee on a weekly basis with women who called me their friend but who haven't had the decency to return my phone calls since calamity came calling.'

He did swear this time.

She transferred her glare to her coffee. 'That was when I decided to be done with all that and focus on something more important.' Her lips lifted. 'Like cupcakes.'

He'd have laughed except he suddenly saw it all too clearly, could see now why she'd done what she had.

'You handed your trust fund, your apartment, and your car over to your father because you wanted to make a clean break with your past.'

'Bingo, tough guy.' She might sound sophisticated

and self-assured, but she couldn't hide the vulnerability that flickered through her eyes. 'Do you think that's stupid of me?'

'I think it was smart and brave. You don't need to be beholden to people like that.'

'Thank you.'

She smiled and for a moment he swore he saw glitter flickering at the edge of his vision. He blinked it away. 'There's one thing I don't get.'

'What's that?'

'Why are you fighting to keep this old relic of a house? Why don't you rid yourself of the responsibility?' And rake in some much-needed moolah while she was at it?

'This house belonged to my grandmother. She's the only person who loved me unconditionally. And she loved this house.'

She wouldn't have wanted it to become an albatross around her granddaughter's neck, surely?

'My parents lived here once they were married, not because it was convenient for the factory but because they wanted to be seen living in the Big House, as you call it. They never loved the place. They look at it and all they see are dollar signs. I look at it and…'

She didn't finish the sentence.

'And you see a Victorian teahouse.'

'You think that's dumb?'

'I think it's an interesting business plan with definite potential.'

She leaned towards him, her face alive. It was the way she'd looked at him fifteen years ago when she'd given him her locket. Only she wasn't a little girl any more but a woman. And he was a grown man.

Heat circled in his veins to pool in his lap. He surreptitiously tried to adjust his jeans, reminding himself about trouble and complications and grief and misery. He was *not* going to travel down that road with Nell. This wasn't a fairy tale. It wouldn't end well. He gritted his teeth. Business—this was just business.

'I've done my homework. High teas have become big business in Sydney. Lots of clients are looking for themed party venues—something a bit different. I think Whittaker House will fit the bill perfectly. I predict my Victorian teahouse will become a big hit, not only for birthday parties, but for hen parties, bridal showers, anniversaries and family reunions too.'

He didn't doubt her for a moment.

'I know Whittaker House isn't Downton Abbey, but it does have its own charm and I happen to think other people would enjoy the location too.'

'Absolutely, but…'

Her face fell. 'But?'

He hated being the voice of reason. 'It'll take a lot of start-up capital to get the business off the ground.' The house would need a lick of paint both inside and out. The grounds would need to be not only wrestled into shape but manicured to within an inch of its life. She'd need to kit out the entire operation with suitable tables and chairs, pretty linens and crockery. It wouldn't come cheap.

'Which is why I'm preparing a business plan to take to my bank manager with projected costs, profits et cetera in the hope I can secure a business loan.'

'Which, unless you have some other asset you've not told me about, will mean putting Whittaker House up as collateral.'

He watched the fire leach out of her eyes. 'How'd you know that?'

It wasn't an accusation but a genuine bid for knowledge. 'I did a business course when I was in prison.'

She chewed her lip and nodded. Her glance sharpened. 'Do you have your own business?'

He shook his head.

'If you're as handy as you say, then maybe you should start up your own building business.'

He choked. 'Me?'

'Why not?'

'There have to be at least a million reasons!'

'And probably just as many why you should,' she said in *that* tone of voice. 'Well, I'm still going to put my proposal together and make an appointment with my bank manager. If I get no joy there then I'll have to find investors.'

'Which means the business is no longer your own.'

'Which isn't ideal, but it's better than nothing.'

He could click his fingers and make the money appear for her. If he wanted. For a moment he was tempted. He cut the thought off. He hadn't told Nell he was rich for the simple reason that he didn't want the news getting about.

She tossed her head. 'I bet there must be some kind of government initiative to assist fledgling businesses. I'll check into that too.'

He had to give her credit. She wasn't sitting around waiting for Prince Charming to swing by and rescue her.

She lifted her chin. 'And if it takes longer to get off the ground than I want, so be it.'

In the meantime she'd be stuck with the upkeep of the place. 'You know your grandmother's rings would bring in the kind of money you need.'

'Out of the question.'

Stubborn. He respected that, but it wouldn't pay the power bills.

She dusted off her hands. 'In the meantime, you're going to do some work on the place in return for rent-free use of the cottage.'

'And cupcakes.'

Her lips twitched. 'And sandwiches and a Sunday roast or two.'

Her eyes narrowed and he recognised the calculation that suddenly flashed in their brilliant green depths. What amendment to their deal would she try and come up with now? He folded his arms and waited.

She moistened her lips. 'If I help you crack that code of John's, would you consider glancing over my business plan once I've written it?'

He grinned. 'Princess, if you can crack that code I'll write the darn plan for you.'

Her hand shot across the table. 'You have yourself a deal.'

He closed his fingers around her hand. His hand completely encompassed hers, but her grip was firm. He didn't want to let go.

'When do you want to move into the cottage?'

He kept hold of it, even though he knew it was dangerous. 'Tomorrow.'

She glanced at the clock. 'Oh, dear Lord!' She pulled her hand from his. 'I'll need to get my skates on if I'm to get it into any fit state to live in.'

'It's fine the way it is, Princess.'

'It most certainly is not!'

'There's absolutely no need to drag your cleaning lady out at this late hour.'

Her head lifted, her chin jutted out—so unconsciously haughty that it couldn't be feigned—and for some reason it made him want to laugh. 'I'll leave the key in the same spot. Will you be able to find it?'

'I'm sure I'll manage.'

Amazingly, she bundled up the remaining cupcakes into brown paper bags. 'Take them home with you.'

'An early down payment?'

'It'll stop me snacking on them. Besides, Tash and Mitch might like one or two.'

He couldn't have said why, but his heart started to burn. He almost did something foolish like invite her to have dinner with him, Tash and Mitch that evening. A crazy, foolish impulse.

Why on earth would the Princess want to have dinner with him? He rose, thanked her for the cupcakes and left.

CHAPTER SIX

RICK HAD JUST finished his last cupcake and a mug of coffee when Nell walked through the back door. She stopped short when she saw him. 'Hey.' She swallowed. 'How's it going?'

Lines fanned out from her eyes and her *frock*—yellow with big purple polka dots—looked rumpled and tired. He wondered what she'd been up to all day. She dropped her handbag on the table, glancing at his plate and mug. Before her face could twist up with suspicion he said, 'You can start using the front door if you like.'

A smile lit through her, banishing the lines around her eyes. 'You fixed it?'

He swallowed. A woman like her could make a man like him feel like Superman if he wasn't careful. 'It was no big deal. The wood had swollen. I filed it back, rehung it and it's as good as new.'

He tried to pull himself back. She might be a damsel in distress…or not. But he was no hero. He knew that and so did she. 'I did promise to earn my keep,' he reminded her.

'Well, yes, but I didn't expect you to start working the moment you moved in. I thought you'd take a day or two to settle in.'

Settle in? It didn't take much 'settling in' to unpack a single suitcase.

'You left cupcakes and sandwiches for me at the cottage.' The cottage had been spotless too—not a speck of dust to be seen. He wondered who she'd had come in and clean it at such late notice.

'Oh, that was just a neighbourly gesture. If I'd thought you'd want to start work today I'd have left you a key.' She stuck out a hip. 'Which rather begs the question—how did you get in?'

His stomach burned acid and he waited for that soul-destroying suspicion to wash over her face, for her to rush off and count the family silver. Ever since he'd been released from jail it was how people treated him. They didn't believe a man could pay his debt to society and then move on and make something of himself.

If he'd known at eighteen what he knew now, would he have still taken the rap for Cheryl, claimed the drugs were his rather than hers? He stared at the Princess and had a feeling that answer would still be yes.

Which meant he hadn't learned a damn thing.

Which meant he was still as big a sucker as he'd ever been.

He'd gone to prison a boy but he'd come out a lot wiser and a whole lot harder. He couldn't draw comparisons between Cheryl and Nell—their lives were too different—but the same protective instincts rose up in him whenever he looked at Nell now.

Ice washed over his skin. He had no intention of getting that close to anyone again—no intention of taking the blame for anything that would land him back in jail. Ever. Regardless of who it was.

'Oh, get over yourself, you idiot!'

He blinked at Nell's rudeness.

'If I trust you with my grandmother's jewels I'm going to trust you with the contents of my house. For heaven's sake, there's nothing left worth stealing anyway. My father long made off with anything of value.'

Genuine irritation rather than suspicion chased across her face and he jolted back into the present. He rolled his shoulders.

'Is my security that bad?'

'It's not brilliant. You should install an alarm system. I, uh, got in through the back door.'

'But I locked it.'

'You need to remember to use the deadbolt.'

She sighed. 'An alarm system? I'd better put it on the list.'

She bustled about making coffee. She eyed the jar of instant he'd bought with distaste. 'Would you like another?'

'No, thanks.'

'Why didn't you make yourself a proper coffee? It's worth the effort, you know.'

'That coffee is yours.'

Very slowly she turned. 'And I'm guessing there's milk in the fridge with your name on it too and sugar in the cupboard?'

He shifted. 'People can get funny about things like that.'

She pointed her teaspoon at him. 'Let's get one thing clear right now.' She raised her voice to be heard above the gurgling of the percolator. 'You're welcome to help yourself to tea, coffee, bread, biscuits and whatever else is in the pantry while you're working. And—' she thrust out her jaw '—if I feel like having instant coffee I mean to help myself to your jar. You have a problem with that?'

He grinned. 'None at all, Princess.'

'Hmph.' She made coffee, sipped it and closed her eyes as if it were the first chance she'd had to relax all day. He wondered again what she'd been up to—hobnobbing with society types hoping to find an investor or three?

'Oh, I meant to ask. Is that your car out front?'

'Yup.'

'There's room to park it in the garage if you want.'

'There's a garage?'

'Come with me.'

With coffee cup in hand, she led him out into the garden. About halfway between the house and the cottage she veered left. Hidden behind strategically placed trees and shrubs squatted a substantial wooden building with three large wooden doors.

She walked across to the cast iron fence, fitted a key into the lock and slid the fence back. The fence slid along on a kind of roller. From the footpath it'd be impossible to see that this part of the fence also acted as a gate.

'I had no idea this was here.' And he must've walked past this section of fence a hundred times. He turned to survey the garage. 'What did that used to be?'

'The stables, once upon a time.' She slid the gate shut again. It barely made a sound. 'They were converted eons ago, which is why the gate and the garage doors aren't automatic. Maybe down the track. Mind you, these big old doors have a certain charm I'd be loath to trade in merely for the sake of convenience.'

She took a sip of coffee. 'This bay here is free.' She lifted a latch and walked backwards until the door stood wide open.

He entered. And then stopped dead. A van, a bit like the ice cream vans that had done the rounds of the neighbourhood during the summers of his childhood, stood in the next bay along. Only, instead of ice creams, the van's sides were decorated with cupcakes. 'Candy's Cupcakes' was written in swirly pastel lettering.

He turned back to her, folded his arms and leant against the doorframe. 'Your business is obviously bigger than I thought.'

She drained her coffee. 'Yes.'

'Why didn't you tell me?'

For a moment her gaze rested on his shoulders. She shook out her arms as if an itch had started up inside her. His heart started pounding to a beat as old as time then too. He gritted his teeth. He and the Princess were not going to dance that particular tango. 'Nell?'

She jumped. 'Sorry, I—'

She averted her face, but that didn't hide the colour on her cheekbones. Rick gritted his teeth harder.

'Sorry.' She turned back. 'I'm tired. Concentration is shot.' She gestured to the van. 'Everyone expects me to fail. Some have said so outright. Some have laughed as if it's a joke. Others have smiled politely while raising sceptical eyebrows. I don't need that kind of negativity in my life.'

'And you thought I'd react that way.'

She met his gaze. 'You did.'

'I…'

'You thought my little cupcake business was limited to a few deliveries on the weekend and nothing more. You didn't even begin to entertain the idea that I might also work Monday to Friday. But I do. I have a weekly schedule and I head out in Candy for the CBD to take cupcakes and coffee to the masses.' She lifted a shoulder and let it drop. 'Or, at least, to office workers. You won't believe the number of people who now treat themselves to a weekly cupcake for morning or afternoon tea.'

Wow.

'I thought you'd know better than to pigeonhole me like you did.'

Everything inside him stilled.

'You've been in jail. I know what people say about you. They think once a criminal always a criminal. They think a man like you can't be trusted and is only out for whatever he can get. And they're still going to think that when your name's cleared because it doesn't change the fact that you were in prison.'

Each word was a knife to the sorest part of him.

'*I* haven't treated you like that.'

She hadn't, but he kept waiting for her to. His stomach started to churn. That was hardly fair, though, was it? She'd shown him nothing but... friendship.

'I also happen to know what people think of me— the pampered society princess who has never had to lift a finger one day in her life.' She strode over and stabbed a finger to his shoulder. 'Well, I'm not useless and I'm not a failure and I'm not...I'm not useless!'

He grabbed the finger that kept jabbing at him and curled his hand around it. 'You're not useless, Princess. You're amazing. Completely amazing and I'm sorry I misjudged you.'

She tried to tug her hand free but he wouldn't let her. 'You really are skint?'

She stopped struggling to frown at him. 'Yes.'

'Yet amid all of your own troubles you've found the time to help me.'

'Help or hound?'

He chuckled and a warmth he'd never experienced washed over him. 'Thank you for cleaning my cottage.'

'You're welcome.'

God, such vulnerability in those wide green eyes, such softness and sweetness beckoned in those lips. She smelt like sugar and frosting and all the things he'd ever longed for. An ache gripped him so hard he had to drag in a breath. 'Princess…' The endearment scraped out of him, raw with need and longing.

She swayed towards him, those green eyes lowering to his lips. The pulse at the base of her throat fluttered faster and faster. Her hand tightened in his.

He gripped her chin and lifted it, needing to taste her so badly he thought he might fall to his knees from the force of it. Desire licked fire through his veins. He moved in close—so close he could taste her breath—but the expression in her eyes froze him.

They glittered. With tears.

'Don't you dare kiss me out of pity.'

She didn't move out of his hold and he knew then she was as caught up in the grip of desire as him.

'Please, Rick. Don't kiss me because you feel sorry for me.'

The tears trembled, but they didn't fall. Every muscle he had screamed a protest, but he released her and stepped back. He swallowed twice before he was sure his voice would work. 'Pity was the last thing on my mind, Princess. So was guilt and feeling apologetic.'

It was just…he'd allowed himself to see her properly for the first time and it had blown him away. He needed to get away from her, to find a sense of balance again. 'I just…' he dragged a hand back through his hair '…I just think it'd be a really bad idea to kiss you.'

'Definitely.'

He glanced at her sharply, but he couldn't see any irony or sarcasm in her face.

She tossed her head. 'Besides, I don't want you or anyone else to think I'm taking advantage of you.'

He almost laughed. 'Take advantage of me?' That'd be the day.

She waved an impatient hand in the air. 'You know what I mean—seducing you so you'll fix up my house all spick and span.' She glared. 'I can stand on my own two feet.'

He glanced at Candy. 'I don't doubt that for a moment.' Did she ever take a day off?

'Right.' She smoothed down her skirt. 'Good. I had some keys cut for you—the front and back doors and the gate here in the fence.'

There was an awkward moment where she held them out to him and he tried to take them and they danced around each other, trying not to touch. In the end she tossed them in the air and he caught them.

'Now, if you don't mind…' She collected her coffee mug from where she'd set it on the ground. 'I'm going to go have a much-needed shower.'

'There's something else we need to talk about, Princess.'

She turned back.

'Those jewels can't stay in the cottage while I'm living there.'

'But—'

'I've been to prison, Nell, and I'm not going back. If those jewels go missing the finger will be pointed at me.'

'Not by me!'

She said that now. 'You need to put them in a safety deposit box, because I'm not risking it.'

The shadows in Rick's eyes told Nell exactly what prison had been like. Oh, not in detail, perhaps, but in essence. She suppressed a shiver. 'I didn't think of that,' she finally said.

When really what she wanted to say was *kiss me, kiss me, kiss me*. Not that kissing would do either one of them any good.

She stroked her fingers down her throat. It might help iron out some kinks…scratch an itch or two.

Oh, stop it! Be sensible.

She cleared her throat. 'Is it okay if I collect them first thing in the morning? As soon as it opens I'll take them to the bank for safekeeping.'

For a moment she thought he might insist on her

taking them now, but eventually he nodded. 'First thing.'

With a nod, she backed out of the garage and fled for the house, leaving him to close up, or to drive his car around, or whatever he pleased.

She sat, planted her elbows on the kitchen table and massaged her temples. Dear Lord, she had to fight this attraction to Rick because he was right—kissing would be a bad, *bad* idea. It'd end in tears—hers. The minute Rick discovered his sibling's identity he'd be out of town so fast she wouldn't see him for dust.

As a kid she'd dreamed of Rick riding up and rescuing her—like the prince rescuing Rapunzel from her tower. That had all been immature fantasising mixed up with guilt, yearning and loneliness. It hadn't been based on any kind of reality.

It hadn't factored in Rick going to jail.

It hadn't factored in that she could, in fact, save herself.

She shot to her feet. 'I am a strong woman who can make her dreams come true.'

She kept repeating that all the way to the shower.

During the next week Nell marvelled at the progress Rick made on the house. He transformed the parlour from something tired and battered into a room gleaming with promise. He'd done something to the fireplace—blackened it, perhaps—that highlighted the fancy tile-work surrounding it. The mantelpiece shone.

It didn't mean they became cosy and buddy-buddy, though. They edged around as if the other were some kind of incendiary device that would explode at the slightest provocation.

When Nell returned home in the afternoons she and Rick would chat—carefully, briefly. Rick would either continue with whatever he was doing or retire to the cottage. She'd start watching one of the spy movies she'd borrowed from the video store or would investigate code breaking on the Internet. To no great effect.

'Oh, for heaven's sake! This is a waste of time.' She slammed down the lid of her laptop. Biting her lip, she reached out to pat it. The last thing she needed was to have to go out and buy a new computer.

'Not having any luck?'

She glanced up to find Rick in the doorway. Wearing a tool belt. Her knees went a bit wonky. She swallowed first to make sure her voice would work. 'I've trawled every website and watched every darn movie ever made about codes and code breaking and yet I'm still none the wiser.' She pulled the piece of paper on which she'd scrawled the code towards her.

'*LCL 217, POAL 163, TSATF 8, AMND 64, ARWAV 33, TMOTF 102,*' she read, even though she'd memorised it.

FREE Merchandise is 'in the Cards' for you!

W

e'd like to send you two free books like the one you are enjoying now. Your two books have a combined price of over $10, but they are yours to keep absolutely FREE! We'll even send you 2 wonderful surprise gifts. You can't lose!

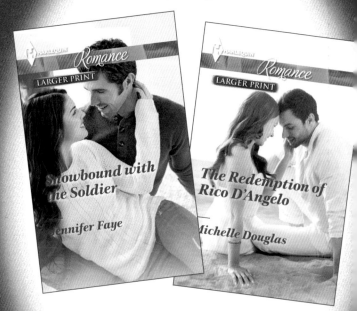

REMEMBER: Your Free Merchandise, consisting of **2 Free Books** and **2 Free Gifts**, is worth over $20.00! No purchase is necessary, so please send for your Free Merchandise today.

Get TWO FREE GIFTS!

We'll also send you two wonderful FREE GIFTS (worth about $10), in addition to your 2 Free books!

Visit us at:

'I don't get it, not one little bit, and I'm tired of feeling stupid!'

He didn't say anything.

She leapt up. It took an effort of will not to kick the table leg. 'Why on earth did he make it so hard?'

'Because he doesn't want me to find the answer.'

'Why tell you at all then?'

'To chase away his guilt? To feel as if he were doing the right thing and giving me some sort of chance at figuring it out?'

To chase away his guilt? In the same way he'd chased Rick away? Her stomach churned. And then she frowned. 'Rick, it's Saturday.'

'Yup.'

'You don't have to work weekends.'

'Why not? You do.'

She blinked.

'I want to attach the new locks I bought for the parlour windows. I've been trying to work that code out all morning and now I want to hammer something.'

She blew out a breath. John's code had evidently left him feeling as frustrated as it had her. 'You haven't given me the receipts for those locks yet.'

His gaze slid away. 'I can't find where I put them. I'll hunt them up tonight and give them to you on Monday.'

That was what he'd said on Wednesday.

'I might not be rolling in money, but I have enough to cover the work you quoted me.' Besides, he couldn't exactly be rolling in it himself. 'Fixing up this house is exactly what I choose to do with my money.' Well, that and eat.

'And I had some questions about the library,' he added as if she hadn't spoken. 'If you have the time…'

Something shifted in the darkness of his eyes, but she couldn't tell what, only that it made her pulse quicken. She scowled. 'Are they questions I'll be able to answer?'

He grinned. It was swift and sudden and slayed her where she stood. 'Colour schemes and stuff.'

She stuck her nose in the air. '*That* I can do. I've been trained by the best. Piece of cake.'

'Speaking of cake…' His gaze searched the table.

She rolled her eyes. 'Yes, yes, there're cupcakes in the cake tin. Help yourself.' It suddenly occurred to her… 'I didn't make you any sandwiches. Would you like me—?'

'Nope, not necessary. Sandwiches Monday to Friday was the deal.'

'Was it?' When he grinned at her like that she forgot her very name and which way was up. She had no hope of recalling anything more complicated. She swung away. 'Nell,' she murmured under her breath. She pointed to the ceiling. 'Up.'

'Talking to yourself, Princess.'

The warm laughter in his voice wrapped around the base of her spine, making her shiver. 'Library,' she muttered instead, pointing and then leading the way through the house.

'It's a nice room,' Rick said from the doorway.

She tried to stop her gaze from gobbling him up where he stood. 'I used to spend a lot of time in here as a child. It was my favourite room.' She hadn't disturbed anyone in here.

'You were a bookworm?'

The look he sent her had her rolling her shoulders. 'Uh-huh.'

He moved into the room. 'Do you mean to keep all of these books in here when you open for business?'

She hadn't thought that far ahead. 'All of the leather-bound collections will probably remain in here—the room wouldn't earn the term library if there were no books.' She trailed her fingers along one wall of glass-enclosed bookcases. 'But I'll take my old worn favourites upstairs. They're a bit tatty now. I suppose I could put some pretty ornaments on the shelves here and there for interest and—'

She stopped dead and just stared.

'What?' Rick spoke sharply and she suspected the blood had all but drained from her face.

'*POAL*,' she managed faintly.

'*POAL 163*,' he corrected.

She opened one of the bookcase doors and dropped to her knees in front of it. She ran a finger along the spines. 'I'd have never got it. Not in a million years.'

'What are you talking about?' He strode across to her, his voice rough and dark. 'Don't play games with me, Nell.'

She grabbed his arm and dragged him down to the floor beside her. 'Look.' She pointed to a book spine.

'*Lady Chatterley's Lover*,' he growled. 'So what?'

'*LCL*.' She pointed to the next spine along. '*Portrait of a Lady—POAL. The Sound and the Fury, A Midsummer Night's Dream, A Room with a View, The Mill on the Floss*. These are my first-year literature texts from university. She pulled out *Lady Chatterley's Lover* and handed it to him. 'Open it at page two hundred and seventeen.'

She had no idea if she were right or not, but…

He turned the pages over with strong, sure hands. They both caught their breath when the page revealed a single sheet of folded paper.

He handed her back the book and she could have sworn his hand trembled. 'It could just be some note or other you made.'

Her heart burned as the conflicting emotions of hope and pessimism warred in his dark eyes. 'It could be,' she agreed, though she didn't think it was. There'd only be one way to find out—if he unfolded it—but she didn't try to hurry him. She couldn't imagine what it must be like to suddenly discover you had a sibling you'd never heard about before.

He leapt to his feet and strode away. She swallowed back the ball of hurt that lodged in her throat. He wasn't obliged to share the contents of John's message with her. She stared instead at the book and waited for him to say something, her heart thumping and her temples pounding.

'A *T.*'

She turned to find him holding up the sheet of paper bearing the single letter. His lips twisted. 'He did say he wasn't going to make it easy, didn't he?'

She gathered up the other five books. 'Obviously it's going to spell something out. Maybe a name.' This room was devoid of any furniture so she took the books back through to the kitchen and set them on the table before walking away.

'Where are you going?'

He spoke sharply and she spun around. 'I thought you might like some privacy.'

He cocked an eyebrow, all tough-guy badness in a blink of his eye. 'Aren't you curious?'

She wished she could say no. 'Of course I am. I'm burning up with it.'

'Then stay. We'd have never got this far if it weren't for you.'

She didn't need any further encouragement. She moved back to the table and watched silently as he laid the six letters out. When he was done they both stood back and stared at it.

THE SUN

A growl left her throat. 'What the bloody hell is that supposed to be and what's all this nonsense of *X, C* and *M* on the last card?'

'Roman numerals,' Rick said, leaning over to look at them more closely. 'I think it's a date.'

He straightened. Nell stiffened. '*The Sun*,' they said at the same time, referring to a Sydney newspaper.

'I'm not good with Roman numerals.' Nell moved back around to her computer. 'But there's bound to be a site on the web that can tell us what that date might be.'

Rick didn't move. 'It's the twenty-sixth of May in the year of two thousand and thirteen.'

That was almost a year ago now. 'The paper is bound to archive its back issues online.' She went to the newspaper's homepage, flicked through several screens and found the paper issued for the twenty-sixth of May. All the while she was aware of Rick standing on the other side of the table, unmoving, and it started to worry her. 'Rick!'

He started and glanced her way. It hit her that inactivity wasn't good for him. 'Here, I found the right paper. I think. You do the search while I organise cake and coffee.'

Searching would keep him focused. Organising afternoon tea would give her something to do with her hands other than fidget.

He took her seat. 'What do you reckon—search the personal classifieds for some coded message?'

She growled. 'It better not be too coded.'

He laughed and turned his attention back to the computer screen.

She measured out coffee and set cupcakes on a plate—Citrus Burst, Pine Lime, Vanilla Cream and Café au Lait. She almost swiped a finger through the frosting of the coffee cupcake, but pulled back at the last minute. It had taken her a lot of work to lose her teenage puppy fat. As soon as she had her Victorian teahouse up and running she meant to enjoy the fruits of her labours to her heart's content and to hell with her waistline. But until then...

Her nose curled. It was a well-known fact that slender women received more chances and better opportunities than plump women. It wasn't fair. In her opinion it was downright scandalous, but she didn't have too many assets—a big house that was threatening to crumble down around her, her ability to cook the best cupcakes on the planet and a trim figure. She meant to make the most of all of them while she could.

Behind her, she sensed Rick's sudden stillness. She swung to him. 'Well?' Her voice came out choked, as if she had an entire cupcake lodged in her throat.

'There's a message here...for me.'

Her heart gave a giant kick. 'Does he tell you...?'

'No. The message reads: *Rick Bradford. Many Happy Returns.*'

The twenty-sixth of May was his birthday?

'*You've exceeded expectations. For she's a jolly good fellow.*'

'She?' That couldn't be right, surely?

'She,' he repeated.

'Do you think that's some oblique way of saying your unknown sibling is a sister?'

'I think he's referring to you.'

Her?

'Return on the thirteenth of March.'

She slammed the plate of cupcakes to the table. 'Return where?' she shouted.

'I think he means to the classifieds in the newspaper.' He leaned back. 'Which means he put some thought into all of this before he died—paid for these ads well in advance. I wonder how many years' worth he organised.'

The intricacy of John's scheme stunned her. 'The thirteenth of March is only a couple of weeks away.' She bared her teeth. 'That is if he's referring to this year. There's no guarantee of that, of course.'

'All will be revealed then if you have the eyes to see it.'

She opened a kitchen cupboard just so she could slam it shut again. 'That's what I think of that!'

'And it ends with *Hip Hip Hooray!*'

'Oh, and that's worth its weight,' she snarled.

He laughed. 'He was right about one thing. You are a jolly good fellow. I'd never have got this far if it hadn't been for you.'

'Well, of course you wouldn't!' she exploded, pacing up and down. 'That's the whole stupid point, isn't it? How could you ever have possibly traced that stupid code to bits of paper in *my* books? How would you have ever known about *my* stupid marigold tin? How dare he risk everything on something so…so tenuous! How could he risk… All of it hangs on such a thin thread that could've broken at any time.' She slashed a hand through the air. 'How could he know I'd keep helping you? How could he know you'd even stick around? How could he know that I hadn't sold the house?'

'He couldn't.'

She stared at the plate of colourful cupcakes and made a fist. Rick dragged the plate towards him out of harm's way.

'Princess, it's not worth getting all hot under the collar about.'

'Not worth…' She started to shake.

'You're really furious at him, aren't you?'

She had a feeling they weren't talking about John any more. 'Yes,' she gritted out. Because whether they were talking about her father or his, it was true on both counts. 'How dare he drag me into his nasty little game!'

Again, that counted on both heads.

'What right did he have? What…'

The air went out of her and she sat with a thump.

Rick leaned towards her, his eyes wary. 'Uh, Nell…you okay?'

She swallowed. 'Earlier you said that he might be trying to make himself feel better…to make amends.'

'Yeah, so?'

'That's what this is about. He wants me to make amends too.'

CHAPTER SEVEN

RICK PULLED UP short when he strode into the kitchen to find Nell drinking coffee and eating cupcakes.

At ten on a Wednesday morning.

He counted two cupcake wrappers, which meant she was steadily making her way through a third. He frowned. That wasn't the way to eat one of those cupcakes! Every mouthful should be savoured to the full.

She didn't look up. He rubbed the back of his neck. 'Good morning.'

She continued to glare at the table. 'Morning.' Bite. Chew. Swallow.

Okay, take two. 'I ducked out to grab a few supplies. I ran out of sugar soap and sandpaper.'

'You don't need to justify your movements, Rick. I believe you'll keep your side of the bargain. The how and when is entirely up to you.'

He should leave her be and get back to sanding and painting, keep it all on a work footing. He hesitated and then pulled out a chair and sat. 'You don't need to justify your movements to me either, but what on earth are you doing at home—' eating cup-cakes as if they were nothing more extraordinary than a digestive '—when peak morning tea time is about to hit Sydney's CBD?'

She ate more cupcake. Her shoulders hunched. 'Candy has broken down.'

He grimaced. 'She's at the garage being repaired?'

More cupcake and more shoulder hunching. 'No.'

'Why not?'

Finally she looked at him. He tried not to wince at the lines of strain that bracketed her mouth. 'Be-cause of these.' She held up a pile of opened letters. 'Bills.' She then proceeded to set each one down onto the table, barking out the amount due. 'It adds up to more than half of what I have left in my ac-count. At the moment I'm not sure I can afford to get Candy fixed.'

Yet without Candy on the road she wouldn't be able to earn the money to pay those bills.

If there was something he'd learned in the last fortnight—other than the fact he really wanted to kiss her—it was that Nell worked like a Trojan. If anyone deserved to cop a break, she did.

'How much money are you expecting to come in from your party orders and how much do you have outstanding?'

She blew out a breath, pushed her plate away and pulled her laptop towards her. 'Let's see…' Her fin-gers danced across the keyboard.

He came around the table to peer over her shoulder. What he saw made him frown. 'Princess, there're half a dozen orders here—' big orders too '—from over three months ago and the bills are still outstanding.'

If her shoulders drooped any further they'd be on a level with the table. He pointed to her spreadsheet. 'Look—here, here and here.' The movement brought him in close so her hair tickled his jaw and the sugar-drenched scent of her made his mouth water. He moved back a few inches to stop himself from doing something stupid. 'These three orders on their own would cover the cost of your bills.'

'I know, but...'

She leapt up and he shot back, dodging her chair before it could do him a serious injury. She paced to the end of the table and then spun back, flinging an arm in the air.

'How do you make people pay? I've sent each of them at least three reminder letters. I've spoken to them on the phone and each time I've been assured the cheque is in the mail. Funny thing is, though, none of those cheques have yet materialised.'

'Do you know if any of these people are in financial difficulties?'

'No! That's the thing. I mean I have written off a couple of debts because I found out...'

She'd written those debts off because she knew what it was like, hadn't she? Because she had an amazing ability to empathise with others—something he'd have never expected in someone from her background. But then he'd misjudged her on so many levels.

It didn't change several salient facts. 'Do you think it's either reasonable or responsible to order a party load of cupcakes if you can't afford it?'

For a long moment she didn't say anything. 'I shudder to think how many bills my father didn't pay.'

'They weren't your responsibility, Princess.' And in the meantime people with the wherewithal to pay took advantage of her. He ground his teeth together.

She merely shrugged. 'You want to know something funny?'

From the tone of her voice he suspected he wasn't going to find whatever it was either amusing or humorous. 'What's that?'

'Each of those people—' she gestured to the computer '—with the outstanding debts; I thought they were my friends.'

It took an effort of will to keep his shoulders loose and relaxed. Two things were certain. Firstly, these people were not friends and secondly, she couldn't afford to write those debts off.

'What you need to do, Princess, is hire a money collector.'

She gazed at him blankly.

'And, as you currently have me at your disposal...'

She stilled. For a glorious moment her eyes gleamed that extraordinary emerald-green that made him want to kiss her all over again. 'Ooh, I couldn't…'

'You have no choice.'

He'd had experience of money collectors from the other side of the fence—they'd visited his mother and grandmother on a too regular basis. But it meant he knew the grim and forbidding demeanour, and he knew how to come across as threatening without actually threatening someone illegally. He'd threaten this lot with exposure in the local paper if they didn't cough up.

She shifted from one foot to the other.

'You worked hard for that money.'

'I know, but…'

'Nell, if you don't have the stomach for this then maybe you need to rethink your plans for Whittaker House.'

She stiffened at that. Without another word she printed off those three bills and handed them to him. He glanced at them and nodded when he saw they contained all the information he needed—names, addresses and amounts outstanding.

'Please don't frighten them.'

'Of course not.' He crossed his fingers behind his back. After he was done they'd think twice before failing to pay a bill again.

'I mean…this will be seriously humiliating for them.'

He'd make sure of it. These people hadn't just humiliated Nell—they'd hurt her, had tried to bully her. They were supposed to be her friends, for goodness' sake!

'And just so you know...' she moistened her lips '...the Fenimores have a Rottweiler.'

He tried not to focus on the shine of her lips. Or on the sweet curve of her lower lip and the way it seemed to swell under his gaze. He snapped away.

This attraction between him and Nell was crazy. It couldn't go anywhere. Acting on it would be a stupid thing to do.

But glorious.

He ignored the insidious voice and tried to concentrate on the conversation. 'Is he vicious?'

'Not in the slightest. He's a big softie. Call their bluff if they...' She lifted a shoulder.

He almost laughed at that, but it wouldn't have been a pretty laugh. He didn't bother telling Nell that he didn't respond well to threats. He'd deal with the Fenimores.

Before he left, however... 'Nell, sit. We need to have a tough talk.'

She eyed him uncertainly, but did as he asked. He knew these bills were merely the tip of Nell's financial troubles. He'd been working on that darn business plan of hers and there wasn't a bank manager in Sydney who'd lend her a red cent unless she put Whittaker House up as collateral. He told her that now in plain unvarnished English.

'But—'

'I'm not telling you this because I want to make

your life difficult, but you need to know the truth.' The panic that raced through her eyes clutched at his heart. 'Nell, I know you loved your grandmother.'

'Yes, of course, but…'

But what did that have to do with anything? He could see the question in her eyes even if she didn't ask it out loud. 'How badly do you want to save Whittaker House? How badly do you want to turn it into a Victorian teahouse?'

She shot to her feet and clenched her hands so hard she shook. 'It's the most important thing in the world to me.'

Because she wanted to honour the memory of the only person who'd shown her unconditional love? Because she wanted to prove she wasn't useless and that she could make a success of her life? Because she had nothing else in her life? *Oh, Princess, you deserve so much more.*

The last thought disturbed him. He shook it off. 'You really want it more than anything?'

'Yes.' Her chin lifted.

Stop thinking about kissing her! 'So you're prepared to make sacrifices?'

'Of course I am!'

His heart grew heavy in his chest. 'You have a source of income that will get you started and keep you out of trouble for a long while. Nell, you need to sell your grandmother's diamond ring.' And probably the emerald as well.

The last of the colour leached from her face. She sat.

He found himself crouching in front of her and clasping her hands. 'It's not a betrayal of your grandmother.'

'Then why does it feel that way?'

'If she were here now, what would she tell you to do?'

'I...'

'Did she place more value on things rather than people?'

'No! She...' She gave a half-laugh full of love... and loss. 'She'd just want me to be happy. If she'd ever had to choose between her diamond ring or this house she'd have sold the ring in an instant.'

He waited and eventually she lifted her chin and squeezed his hands. 'You're right. It's time to be practical. My grandmother's spirit doesn't reside in a few pieces of jewellery.'

He stood and moved back. Holding Nell's hand when she was upset was one thing. Holding it when she fired back to life was altogether different.

Different and compelling and bewitching.

'Besides, those jewels would've been more trouble than they're worth. I'd have had to be constantly looking over my shoulder waiting for my father to try and take them.'

Rick had grown up among people like that, but it made his gut clench that the Princess had experienced it too.

'For heaven's sake, look at me! Sitting around here comfort eating and feeling sorry for myself. How pathetic!'

She was a lot of things, but pathetic wasn't one of them.

He shifted his weight. 'If someone offered you a pot of gold to get you out of this fix…and it'd mean you'd get to keep your grandmother's rings, would you accept it?'

She bit her lip and then shook her head. 'No.'

He breathed easier.

'I want to do this under my own steam.'

Good.

'So while you go and play bailiff I'm going to get my grandmother's ring out of the safety deposit box and make an appointment with a jewellery evaluator. An antique piece like that…it might even be worth placing in an auction.'

A coil of tension in his chest loosened at the colour in her cheeks and the sparkle in her eyes. *Way to go, Princess.*

'I think it might be a good idea for me to attend that appointment with you.'

She stared at him and then a Cheshire cat grin slanted across her face. 'While I have absolutely no intention of being taken advantage of, I think that's an excellent plan. I dare anyone to even think of it while you have my back.'

Exactly. 'I'll see you back here in a couple of hours.'

'Won't you need more time?'

The addresses were all within twenty minutes of Nell's house. 'I don't think so.' He made for the door.

'Rick.' She bit her lip. 'Don't let any of them make you feel like a second-class citizen. You have more true honour in your pinkie finger than any of them have in their entire bodies.'

Something inside him expanded. He couldn't utter a word.

'And you—you who have every reason to bear me a grudge—have shown me more true friendship than just about anyone.'

As she spoke she moved towards him. All he could do was watch. Common sense told him to back up, but his feet refused to move. Reaching up on tiptoe, she kissed his cheek, drenching him in all of her sweetness. A groan rose in his throat, but he swallowed it back.

'Thank you.'

The sincerity of it shook him loose. 'No sweat, Princess.' He had to break the moment or something would happen—something earth-shattering that had the potential to break both of them.

It doesn't have to.

But it would. Guys like him didn't end up with girls like her.

He cleared his throat. 'I don't suppose you could spare a cupcake or two for a hardworking bailiff on his weary travels?'

She laughed at that, retrieved a large cardboard

box of them and pushed it into his hands. 'Maybe you could leave one with each of them as a gesture of…goodwill.'

He grinned. 'Behind that pretty face you're evil, you know?'

She blinked.

'Because we both know one cupcake is never enough.'

That slow smile spread across her face again. 'Give them hell, Rick.'

He tipped an imaginary hat at her and left. He fully intended to.

Rick returned to find Nell waiting for him. She immediately leapt up to put the kettle on to boil. 'How did it go? Were they horrible to you? Did they say mean things to you?'

Not: *Did you get my money?* Not: *Was the mission successful?* But: *Were they horrible to you?* He stopped dead and just stared.

Her face darkened. 'They were.' He watched in a kind of bemusement as her hands clenched. 'I'm sorry! I shouldn't have asked that of you. I should've done my own dirty work and—'

'I had a ball.'

She eyed him warily. 'You did?' she finally ventured.

He could see she didn't believe him. 'Ever since I got out of jail, people like those clients of yours have made me feel like scum. I can't tell you how satisfying it was to turn the tables. Do you have any more outstanding debts I can deal with?'

That surprised a laugh out of her—as it was meant to. She pushed him into a chair, set a plate of sandwiches in front of him and grabbed him a beer. 'One thing's for sure. You've earned lunch.'

She stood over him then with arms folded. He glanced up, a sandwich halted halfway to his mouth. 'What?'

'I don't think you should let anyone make you feel like scum.'

That was easier said than done, but... It struck him then that Nell had only ever treated him as an equal—someone deserving of respect and consideration.

The realisation tightened his chest. He bit into the sandwich then took a swig of his beer. Neither loosened the tension growing inside him. He pulled three cheques from his pocket and handed them to her.

She flicked through them and her eyes widened. 'You managed to get them to sign cheques for the *entire* amounts outstanding?'

He wanted to puff out his chest at the delight bubbling up through her. 'What were you expecting?'

'More promises. Part payment at best.' She perched on a chair across the table from him and crossed a leg. 'It couldn't have been easy.'

'Princess, it was a piece of cake.'

Nell stared at him. It might've been simple for him, but there was no way on God's green she'd have been able to manage this same outcome. She checked the amount on the cheques again. 'This is amazing.'

He was amazing.

'This will keep the wolf from the door for a little while.' Enough to give her some breathing space at least.

'Were you really friends with those people?'

Some of the golden delight leached out of her. 'I thought we were.' If a single one of those people had found themselves in the same desperate financial straits that she had, she wouldn't have dropped them. She might not have been able to give them financial aid, but she'd have offered them moral support. She'd—

'Princess?'

She snapped to. Although she tried to keep her face composed she couldn't stop her lips from twisting. 'It seems my entire life has been a series of very poor judgement calls.' Letting her parents browbeat her into saying Rick had taken her locket; working so hard to earn her parents' love and approval to discover that they'd never been worth the effort, that they didn't know the meaning of the word love; spending her free time with people who only liked her when she was successful—shallow, callous people who enjoyed playing power games with those less fortunate than themselves.

It wasn't noble, but… 'I hope you gave them a seriously hard time.'

'I can assure you that they didn't enjoy the experience.'

The warmth in his eyes almost undid her. She leapt up to pour herself a glass of water. 'Oh, here.' She pulled a velvet pouch from her handbag. 'My grandmother's ring. You might like to keep a hold of it.'

'No.'

She frowned. 'I thought you were going to be my muscle, my brawn…my hard man.' It'd be safer with him than with her.

'You keep hold of the ring and I'll guard you.' There wasn't an ounce of compromise in his eyes. Slowly she pocketed it again, recalling his words when he'd demanded the jewels be removed from the cottage. *I've been to prison, Nell, and I'm not going back.*

Bile churned in her stomach. Jail must've been hell. Pure hell. She wished he'd been spared that.

'Did you make an appointment for a valuation?'

'Yes, we're to meet with the evaluator in an hour.'

He stopped eating to stare at her. It felt as if his gaze reached right down into her soul. She swallowed and wanted to look away, but she couldn't. 'You sure you're okay with this?' he said.

Was he afraid she'd become hysterical partway through negotiations?

'I wish things could be otherwise, but that's just not possible. So, yes, I'm okay with this.'

And because she didn't want him to read any of

the other thoughts rising up through her, she backed towards the hallway. 'I'll just go powder my nose and get ready.'

He didn't call anything teasing after her and she wondered if he'd read her thoughts despite her best efforts. Thoughts of kissing him, of the need that pummelled her whenever he was near...of how close she'd come earlier to throwing herself at him.

Oh, that would've been another sterling example of her brilliant judgement. Rick might want her. She knew enough to know what the heat in his eyes meant when he looked at her a certain way. She knew that these days men found her attractive. And she knew she found Rick attractive, but where would it lead? To heartbreak, that was where.

Rick wasn't a criminal, but he was a heartbreaker. He'd made it clear that he had no intention of sticking around once he solved the mystery his father had set him. And she didn't fool herself that she'd be the woman to change his mind.

She was through with fairy tales. From here on she dealt in reality.

'I'm sorry, Ms Smythe-Whittaker, but this ring is a copy...a fake.'

The room spun, the ground beneath her feet bucked, and Nell had to reach out and grip the countertop in front of her.

'Mind you, it's a very good copy. It wouldn't have been cheap to have had this made.' The jeweller peered at the ring through his eyeglass again. 'But there's no doubt about it. The stone is just a very cleverly cut crystal and not a diamond.'

It was Rick's hand at her elbow that finally stopped the room from spinning. It took all her strength, but she gathered the shreds of her composure around her. 'How disappointing.'

'I am sorry, Ms Smythe-Whittaker.'

'I am too, but I do thank you for taking the time to look at it. I can't tell you how much I appreciate it.'

He handed her the ring. 'Any time. It's been a pleasure.'

Nell, with a silent Rick at her back, left the shop.

'Could he have been mistaken…or lying?'

She shook her head. 'The man has an impeccable reputation. He would never consider taking a bribe from my father to suggest the ring was a fake. He wouldn't risk his professional standing like that.'

'Nell—'

'Please, not here. Let's wait till we get home.' A home she might not be able to keep for much longer. A lump lodged in her throat. She swallowed, but that only shifted the heaviness to her chest.

Could she give up the idea of her gorgeous Victorian high teas and get a real job?

Doing what? Who would employ her? And even if she could get a job, the likelihood of making a wage that could manage the upkeep of Whittaker House was so slim as to be laughable.

She didn't realise they'd reached home until she

found herself pushed into a chair with a glass of something foul-smelling pressed into her hand. 'Drink,' Rick ordered.

Obeying was easier than arguing. She tipped the glass back and swallowed the contents whole.

'Omigod!' She gasped for air. She choked and coughed and struggled to breathe.

'That's better.'

'Better? What are you trying to do? Poison me!'

'You've at least some colour in your cheeks again.'

She bit her lip. *Dear Lord...* 'Have I gone pathetic again?'

'There's nothing pathetic about you, Princess. You've just had a nasty shock.'

She held her glass back out to him. 'May I have another one of those? It was very…bracing.'

He took the glass with a laugh and handed her a soda instead.

'I see we're being sensible now,' she grumbled.

'If you want to get roaring drunk we'll need to find you something better than cooking brandy.'

He had a point. Besides, she didn't want to get roaring drunk. Not really. She hunched over her can of soda, twirling it around and around on the spot.

'So…obviously my father ransacked the jewels before John hid the box.'

'But why have a copy made? Why go to that bother?'

She stared at him. 'That's true. He didn't go to the same trouble for the diamond necklace, did he?'

'Unless John moved the box before he had a chance to.'

She turned the question over in her mind. 'No,' she finally said. 'He wouldn't go to that effort just for me. He'd simply laugh as if he'd bettered me, got one up on me. He'd tell me to suck it up.'

On the table Rick's hand clenched. 'I'm fairly certain I don't like your father.'

Ditto.

She blew out a breath. 'He must've pawned that ring while my grandmother was still alive. He's not afraid of me, but he'd have been afraid of her retribution.' She twirled her can around a few more times, running a finger through the condensation that formed around it. 'Which means I'd better not pin my hopes on anything else in that box.'

'Nell…'

She glanced up at the tone of his voice. She immediately straightened at the expression on his face. 'What's wrong?'

'You're aware that I had both the means and the opportunity to take something from that jewellery box and to have had a copy made.'

'Oh, right, in all of your spare time in the what— one night it stayed there?'

'I knew about it for two nights.'

She folded her arms. All the better to resist the urge to pitch her soda at him. 'I've already told you more than once that I don't believe you're a thief. How many more times do I have to say it before you believe me?' If her glare could blister paint, the wall behind him should be peeling by now. 'Why are you so determined for me to think badly of you?'

He dragged a hand down his face and her chest cramped and started to ache. He *didn't* want her to think badly of him, but he kept expecting her to because that was how people treated him. She didn't blame him for this particular chip on his shoulder, but she wasn't 'people'.

He held up a hand to forestall her. 'If a complaint were made, I'd be a major suspect.'

'Oh, for heaven's sake, who's going to make a complaint? I can assure you that I won't.' Though it'd serve her father right if she did and the scandal was splashed all over the papers. But it wouldn't bring Grandma's ring back. 'And the only other interested party—my grandmother—is dead. I think you can rest easy on that head, don't you?'

He sat back as if she'd punched the air out of him. 'You really believe I'm not a thief.'

She pulled out her most supercilious shrug. 'I refuse to repeat myself on that head ever again.'

He laughed. 'You're an extraordinary woman, you know that?'

'Uh-huh, extraordinary and broke.'

He grinned, a sexy devil of a smile that made her heart lurch and her pulse beat like a crazy thing. She should look away, be sensible, but it seemed as if the fire from the brandy had seeped into her blood.

'Would you like a cupcake?' she offered.

'I'd love one, but I better not. You'd read me the riot act if I told you how many of those things I've eaten today.'

'With Candy breaking down, it's not like I didn't have plenty to spare,' she mumbled.

His grin only widened.

'Oh, okay!' she snapped. 'I'll take the bait. How come are you so darn happy when my life is imploding around me?'

He leaned towards her. 'Let me lend you the money, Nell.'

Her jaw dropped.

'I have the funds. Doing your business plan, I've calculated how much you need.' He named a sum. 'I've more than enough in the kitty to cover it.'

Her jaw dropped lower.

'And, believe me, if there's one person who can make a success out of a crazy Victorian teahouse, then, Princess, that person is you.'

CHAPTER EIGHT

NELL STARED AT RICK. For a moment she didn't know what to say. She moistened her lips. 'I can't let you risk your money like that.'

'Taking risks is how I've made my money. As far as I'm concerned, this is the safest risk I've taken with it so far.'

Did he mean that? For some reason his certainty only brought her insecurities rushing to the surface. 'You can't know that! You can't know that I'll pull this off. It may all end in disaster and—'

'I've yet to meet anyone who works as hard as you.'

His dark eyes fixed on her with an intensity that dried her mouth and sent her heart twirling and jumping with the kind of exuberance that made it impossible to catch her breath.

He rose, went to the sideboard and pulled the file containing all her clippings and notes from a drawer. 'I stumbled across this last week. I wasn't snooping. I was looking for string.'

She swallowed and pointed. 'Next drawer along.'

'I know that now.'

She stared at the folder and shrugged. 'That's just a whole bunch of pictures and ideas I've collected and...' She trailed off.

He reached across the table and took her hand. 'It's a whole lot more than that.'

Okay, there were recipes and menus and table settings and names of businesses she might be able to use. There were colour schemes for Victorian houses, teapots, and anything else that had taken her fancy that she thought might prove inspirational for her own venture. She'd have to get a bigger folder soon because that one was bursting at the seams and she was adding to it all the time.

'This helped me visualise your dream.'

His hand on hers was warm and it seemed to be melting her from the inside out.

'Rick, I—'

'It made me see your Victorian teahouse wasn't some last-ditch plan to save your skin, but...'

She tried to pull her hand away, but his grip only tightened. 'Nell?'

She couldn't resist him. Not when he said her name like that. She lifted her gaze to his.

'This is a dream of long standing. It's something you've thought long and hard about. You have the drive and the work ethic to make a success of this business.'

His thumb stroked her wrist in lazy circles. She wanted to stretch and purr at his touch.

'I'm cynical enough to know that's not necessarily a recipe for success.'

'Well, of course not,' she said, because she had to say something and that slow circling of his thumb was addling her brain.

'But you have an X factor.'

His thumb stopped its stroking and the cessation added weight to his words.

'An X factor?' *What on earth...?* Had he had too much sun today?

'Talent.'

Everything inside her stilled.

'Your cupcakes could make grown men weep.'

'Oh, anyone can learn to do that.' She pulled her hand from his to wave it in the air. She'd reclaimed it deliberately. Rick was treading on her dreams—admittedly very carefully—but if he suddenly became lead-footed she wasn't sure she could bear it.

He shook his head. 'Nobody makes cupcakes like you. Why are you determined to dismiss that as if it's of little value?'

Not holding his hand didn't help at all. She reached across the table to lace her fingers through his. 'The thing is, Rick, it doesn't actually seem like much. After twenty-five years of privileged living it seems the only talent I've acquired is to make cupcakes. I know they're pretty good, but...' She shrugged. As much as she tried to channel nonchalance, she'd never felt more naked in her life.

'They're not just good. They're spectacular.

They're the kind of cupcakes people travel hundreds of kilometres for.'

She laughed. 'Now you're just being silly.'

'And you're wrong. You're good at lots of things. You're running your own small business, aren't you?'

'Not very successfully if today is anything to go by.'

'You troubleshot that.'

He'd troubleshot that.

'You have social poise and that's rarer than you know. It'll hold you in good stead as the face of the business when the teahouse is up and running—you'll need it. You also have vision and courage and you're not afraid of hard work or sacrifice.'

She opened her mouth, but he held up a hand to forestall her. 'Sorry, Princess, but you're not going to talk me out of believing in you.'

Unconsciously, her hand tightened in his. 'You believe in me?' she whispered.

'Heart and soul.'

Her heart leapt.

'I believe in you so much I'm willing to lay out the money you need to get your business off the ground.'

A lump the size of a teapot lodged in her throat. Nobody had ever told her they believed in her before.

'So will you accept my loan and make this dream of yours a reality?'

She really wanted to say yes, but the lump refused to dislodge. She stared at him and his face gentled as if he could read what was on her mind. He reached out his fingers as if to touch her cheek. She held her breath…

He snapped away.

They shook their hands free.

Bad idea. Touching of any kind. They both knew it was a bad idea.

'I'd best warn you, though, that there'll be some stipulations that come with the loan.'

Finally she was able to harness the strength to swallow deeply enough to clear her throat. 'Like?'

'It won't be interest free.'

'Of course not!'

Though she had a feeling that was just a sop thrown to her pride. Still… 'This can't be charity, Rick. It's business. I will be paying you back at business loan interest rates.'

'You bet it's business and I want it to succeed. It's in my best interests that it succeeds, which is why I want you to drop back to three days on the road with Candy.'

'But—'

'You need to start focusing some real energy on the new venture or call it quits right now.'

'I…'

'Between your weekend orders and three days out in Candy, you'll still be making enough to live on while you get Whittaker House ready. Your personal expenses are incredibly low…for a princess.'

They both knew her living expenses were incredibly low full stop. Circumstances demanded it. He might call her a princess but she lived like a pauper in her rundown castle.

'And you'll have the loan to cover the larger expenses like land rates and power bills.'

He was taking a risk and he was demanding that she take a risk too.

'Well?'

Her heart thumped. 'Yes, thank you, Rick. I would very much like to accept your offer.'

When Nell reached out a hand Rick shook it. He didn't keep hold of it like he wanted, though. The more time he spent in her company the more he wanted to touch her.

You only need to hold out for another couple of weeks. Once he found out the identity of his sibling he'd leave.

And go where?

Who cared? Just somewhere different where the people didn't know him, where they didn't whisper behind his back.

Nell's not like that.

Yeah, but Nell was one in a million. The fierce gladness that had gripped him when she'd accepted his offer of a loan, though, had taken him off guard.

But...

It was just...

The Princess deserved a break.

He leaned back in his chair, assumed his usual

swagger. 'I'll organise to have the funds transferred into your account early next week.'

She peered down her nose at him. 'You need to have a contract drawn up.'

Whatever. He trusted her. His grin widened when she didn't ask the question he could see burning in her face. 'You're just dying of curiosity, aren't you?'

She lifted her chin. 'I have no idea what you're talking about.'

He laughed. 'You want to know how I came to have so much money.'

He watched her manners wrestle with her curiosity.

'Okay, you win. Yes, I do. I want to know how you came to have so much money that you can offer to help…' her lips twisted '…damsels.'

'You're no damsel, Princess. If you were some helpless woman looking for a man to make it all right I wouldn't still be here. Damsels are afraid of independence, hard work and taking risks. None of those things apply to you.'

She leaned back and folded her arms. 'It doesn't answer the question of how you made your money, though, does it? Or why you live even more cheaply than I do.' She frowned. 'Are you lending me all of your money?'

'No.'

Behind the glorious green of her eyes her mind raced. 'Have you left yourself enough money to cover emergencies and the like if they crop up?'

'Yes.'

She pursed her lips and he almost laughed out loud when he realised she didn't believe him. Did she really think he'd be as Sir Galahad as all that? The thought had him shifting on his chair.

'What percentage of your savings have you just lent me?'

And because he could see she was on the brink of pulling back he told her the truth. 'About five per cent.' And that was a conservative estimate. He had so much money he found it hard to keep specific figures in mind.

She stared. She seized a pen and piece of paper and did the maths. She held up the amount she came up with.

'That'd be about right.'

'You're a millionaire. Several times over.'

It wasn't a question so he didn't say anything.

She blew out a breath. 'That's a relief. I can stop worrying that I'll be leaving you short.'

Something muddied the green of her eyes. For reasons he couldn't begin to explain, a bad taste coated his tongue. Was she going to try to hit him up for more money? Would she—

'I'm glad you have money.' Those incredible eyes met his. 'How did you do it?'

Her surprise rankled. 'Shocked?' he taunted.

'To the soles of my feet,' she returned, evidently undaunted by his glare.

'Not to be expected of the jailbird?'

She maintained his gaze and it was so steady it made his heart thump. 'You're the one who keeps reminding everyone that you were in jail.'

Yeah, well, it was better to get in first than be taken by surprise when your guard was down.

'And you never qualify it with the fact your name has been cleared.' She frowned then glared. 'What is that about?'

Her question hit too closely to the sore spots inside him. 'When I was in prison a fellow inmate taught me how to count cards.'

Her eyes turned a murky green like a sea churned up by a storm. 'Was it horrible?' she whispered. 'Prison, I mean. Was it awful?'

Nobody had ever asked him that before. Nobody. And it ripped all his defences from him.

'Rick?'

The sympathy in her eyes, the care in her face, tore something in him. 'It was worse than awful.' The words burst from him before he could stop them. She reached out with both of her hands to grip one of his. 'There are men in there so terrifying they freeze your blood. I didn't think I would get out of that place alive.'

Memories, dark and powerful, pounded at him, one after the other. He rested his head on his free hand and gripped Nell's hands tightly, ordered himself to keep breathing. 'The things you have to do in there to survive… I thought anything in me that was good and kind would be gone for good.'

'But that didn't happen.'

That was when he realised her touch anchored him. He lifted his head and met her gaze. 'I'm not convinced about that, Princess.'

'I am.'

Her belief pushed back some of the darkness. 'How can you be so sure?'

'Tash is still friends with you. She wouldn't be if you'd changed that much. You've been kind to me. You want me to have the opportunity to follow my dream. Someone with no good left in them wouldn't care about that. And someone with nothing good or kind in them wouldn't care if they had ten unknown siblings who needed them or not.'

'I don't know if I do care about that yet.'

'You care enough to find out what their circumstances are like.'

His heart thumped.

Her gaze refused to release his. 'I'm sorry you went to prison. I'm sorry you had to suffer through all of the horror of it. But, whatever else you believe, know this. It didn't destroy who you are. It didn't destroy your honour and integrity. It didn't even destroy your sense of humour or your ability to appreciate the little things. I don't doubt that prison left you with scars, but you're a man in a million and don't let the naysayers convince you otherwise.'

He wanted to believe her with everything he had. He pulled in a breath, unable to deal with all of the confusion raging through him, the pain of remembering that time and all it had stolen from him. He pushed it all away to some deep inner depth where he hoped it'd never see the light of day again. 'I guess it did have its silver lining.'

She choked. 'I beg your pardon?'

'Like I said, I learned to count cards. When I was released from jail I was hired by a building firm. It was one of those parole programmes the powers that be are so gung-ho for. Anyway, I took my first pay packet to the casino and trebled it. Next fortnight I did the same. Within six months I'd made ten times my original winnings.'

'You made your money gambling?'

'I moved from one form of gambling to another. Once I had enough money I traded in blackjack for the stock market. I started making some decent investments, took some risks which paid off.'

'Where did you learn about the stock market?'

'One of the benefits of prison is access to education. I did a business course. Like I said, silver linings.'

Nell leapt up, poured herself a glass of water and drained it. 'You're saying that if it wasn't for prison you wouldn't be rich.'

'That's exactly what I'm saying.'

'What do you think your life would've been like if you hadn't gone to jail?'

He shrugged. 'I'd have ended up working in your father's glass factory or one of the auto parts factories. I'd probably have played on the local football team and I guess I'd have eventually settled down—got married and had a couple of kids.'

She stared down into her glass. 'That sounds kind of nice.'

Yeah, it did.

'But you speak as if none of that's possible now.'

It wasn't.

'You have all this money and yet this is how you choose to live—drifting around like a vagrant as if you don't have two dimes to rub together?'

'I'm not hurting anyone.'

She stared at him. Eventually she nodded. 'You're a good man, Rick—you're kind and you'd rather help than hinder—but prison did steal something from you.'

He stiffened. 'You want to explain that?'

'It stole your courage.'

His head snapped back.

'Before you went to jail you had dreams. Now...' She shrugged. 'Now you're too scared to dream.'

Her words sliced through him.

'Because if you did, you wouldn't choose to live your life the way you do.'

A film of ice covered him from head to foot. 'How I live my life is no concern of yours.' He stabbed a finger at her for added emphasis. 'It's no business of yours.'

Nell shrugged as if his coldness couldn't touch her. 'You're a hypocrite too.' She turned away to wash the dishes in the sink.

His jaw dropped, but he doubted she'd noticed. 'I'm lending you a ludicrous amount of money and all I get is abuse?'

She glanced over her shoulder and raised an eyebrow. 'You want me all doe-eyed and grateful?'

Actually, if he were honest, he wanted her hot and sweaty and horizontal.

'I don't think so,' she snorted. 'I have a feeling doe-eyed would have you running for the hills, tough guy.'

He ran a finger around the collar of his shirt.

'If you intend to concern yourself with my affairs then you can jolly well put up with me concerning myself with yours.'

He thrust out his jaw. 'I'll take back that offer of a loan.'

She turned and planted sudsy hands on her hips. They made damp patches on her dress and he found it hard to look away. 'Go on then,' she said.

He opened his mouth. He stared at those sudsy hands and swore. Nell merely laughed. 'You can't because you're too nice a man.'

Nobody called him nice.

'It's called friendship, Rick.'

He stilled. She went back to washing the last of the dishes. Friendship. Had the Princess just offered him friendship?

Actually, he saw now that she'd offered it the moment he'd shared John's letter with her.

Back-alley guys like him didn't end up with uptown girls like the Princess, but… But it didn't mean they couldn't be friends, did it?

He rolled his shoulders. He stretched his neck first one way then the other. 'You never told me what was wrong with Candy.'

She pulled the plug and reached for a tea towel. 'The roadside assistance guy who got me started again said something about…points and plugs? Are they something that belong in a car?'

He bit back a grin. 'Yep.'

'Well, apparently they need replacing and so does my…alternator?'

She asked the last as if checking she had that word right too.

'Is that all?' His shoulders rolled suddenly free. 'I can fix that for you. I'll need to grab some parts, but all up it should cost less than two hundred dollars. Mind you, the shop would charge four times that to cover labour.'

She tossed the tea towel and slammed her hands to her hips again. 'Is there anything you can't do?'

He found himself laughing. Nell made him feel young—young and alive and free. 'You can deal with sleazy solicitors and smarmy estate agents and I can debt collect and fix cars.'

'You haven't seen under Candy's hood. What makes you so sure you can fix her?'

'I spent a ludicrous amount of time in my mis-spent youth with the guys in the neighbourhood trying to keep our rust-bucket cars on the road. I even helped restore a couple.'

She took a step towards him, her face alive. 'From scratch?' He nodded and her smile widened. 'What fun!'

The Princess was interested in cars? 'C'mon—' he hitched his head in the direction of the door '—let's go take a look.'

When they reached the garage, Rick popped Candy's bonnet. 'Tell me what you know about the engine.'

She wrinkled her nose. 'I'm afraid it's not much.'

She looked so pretty in her 1950s-style dress and heels peering into the workings of the old van it was all he could do not to kiss her. 'That doesn't matter.'

'I don't know what any of it does, but I know that's where I put in water if it's running low.' She touched the radiator cap. 'And that's where I put in the oil.'

'You put in your own oil?'

'A man at the garage showed me how. It's a cinch. Way easier than making cupcakes.'

All he could do was stare.

'So what are plugs and points and an alternator? What do they do?'

He pulled off the distributor cap and pointed to the plugs and points and explained how they worked. She asked questions—intelligent questions—and before he knew what they were about they'd dismantled the alternator from the van and had it spread on the floor of the garage.

'It's fascinating!'

She went to brush a strand of hair from her face, but he caught hold of her hand before she could. He turned it over and pointed. 'I'm thinking you don't want to smear grease all over your face or through your hair.'

She stared at both of her hands in astonishment. 'Heavens, this is messier than gardening…and just as much fun.'

The grin she shot him almost slayed him where he crouched.

'I think it'd be wonderful to be able to repair a car.'

'I can teach you how to change plugs and points. When we get a new alternator I'll show you how to install it. And if you want I'll even teach you how to do a grease and oil change. I warn you, though, it's a mucky business.'

Nell stared at Rick and was almost too afraid to breathe. 'You will? Really truly?'

'Sure I will.'

She'd get covered in grease, she'd break fingernails, and it'd be one more step towards becoming independent and not useless.

And it'd be fun!

It hit her then that she'd been so busy trying to plug all the holes in her life that she'd forgotten about fun.

She couldn't stop herself from beaming at Rick. 'Thank you!'

He grinned that slow grin that could turn a woman's world upside down. Her heart pounded up into her throat and back again to bam-bam in her chest and she couldn't have reached into her wardrobe of shrugs and pulled one on now for all the money in the Reserve Bank.

She didn't care about shrugs. She cared about learning new things and making a success of her life and…

And she cared about Rick.

As a friend.

Somewhere inside her a metaphorical eyebrow lifted. She swallowed and glanced back over at him. His smile had faded. Those dark eyes fixed on her with an intensity that froze everything—even the air—and then it all rushed back, wind roaring in her ears, and she swayed.

Rick reached out to steady her, but she shot to her feet and stumbled. He rose too—as if attached to her by some invisible string—and again he reached out a hand to steady her. 'You're a bit wobbly on your feet there, Princess.'

She didn't know if it were the touch on her arm or the way his teasing swagger didn't quite reach his eyes, but the ability to lie had deserted her. Either that or she'd flung it away recklessly. And she hadn't done anything reckless in fifteen years.

'I've been off balance ever since I saw you standing on my front veranda, Rick.'

All signs of teasing fled. 'Princess...'

One of his fingers slid up her arm. She glanced down at it. 'That's not helping.' But the finger didn't stop—it moved back down from her elbow to her wrist, tracing a path along the inside of her arm.

She wanted to dash herself against him like a wave against a rock and encompass him completely. And still that finger trailed paths of spiralling heat and delight across her skin.

'That makes both of us, Princess, because I find it hard to remember my own name when I'm around you.'

They'd cast pretence aside. She lifted her chin. 'I know you find me attractive sometimes.'

'All the time.'

'And I know there's a lot of reasons why I shouldn't kiss you and you shouldn't kiss me.'

'Uh-huh.'

'But I can't remember any of them at the moment so you better start reciting them to me, Rick, because...'

'Because?'

They moved an inch closer to each other. 'Because kissing you is the only thing I can think of.'

They reached for each other...and stopped at the same time. Nell glanced at her greasy hands. Rick glanced at his. She didn't want to ruin his shirt, but... 'I don't care about my dress,' she whispered.

His mouth hooked up in *that* way. 'But I like that dress. The things I dream of doing to you while you're wearing that dress would make you blush, Princess.'

She hadn't known her heart could beat any harder. She hadn't known her skin could flare with so much heat.

'I care about the dress...' But his words emerged on a rough growl and they wrapped around the base of her spine until she trembled with the force of it.

His hand reached for hers, their fingers lacing. One tug brought them chest to chest. He glanced down at her and his eyes darkened. Very slowly she slid against him, relishing the feel of his hard chest against her softness.

His quick intake of breath curled her toes. 'It seems we don't need hands,' he murmured.

His thumb brushed against the sensitive pulse point of her wrist. Very slowly she turned her hands so his spooned them before dancing her fingers across the backs of his fingers and then lacing them through his again. 'I like hands.' The words came out on short, jerky breaths.

His hands tightened about hers. She tried to glance up at him, but her gaze caught on the pulse pounding at the base of his jaw. She ached to touch her lips to the spot. She wanted—

'Princess?'

She looked up at his hoarse rasp.

Very slowly his lips descended towards hers. She

held his hands tightly as the world tilted and, leaning her weight against him, she reached up on tiptoe to help close the distance between them.

And finally their lips touched.

CHAPTER NINE

THEIR LIPS TOUCHED, their mouths opened, and the world spun away from Nell as the taste and feel of Rick filled her. The only thing that mattered was the way his mouth moved over hers—tender but firm, slow yet sure, practised but with a hint of tentativeness that spoke of his desire to please. It told her that the same stunned delirium that coursed through her veins coursed through his.

He nibbled her bottom lip and she moaned, arching against him, feeling anything might be possible in this moment, feeling she could be anything she wanted to be in this moment and that would be okay.

His lips slanted over hers again, less tentative, more urgent, and she met him kiss for kiss, deepening it at the same moment that he did—tongues dancing, teasing, awakening.

She'd thought he'd taste dark and dangerous… like the shadows she sometimes saw in his eyes, but he tasted like cupcakes—all vanilla and spice— and her sweet tooth sat up and begged. He tasted of every good thing she'd never had in her life before.

He tasted of all the good things she wanted to be in her life—smart, capable, competent. He tasted like…life.

She wanted to crawl inside his skin or to pull him inside hers. He kissed her back as if he wanted that too. They kissed until they had no oxygen left and then very slowly they eased away from each other, fingers still entwined.

She touched her tongue to her bottom lip and sucked it into her mouth. He watched with those dark eyes. 'Wow, that was something,' she said when she could finally speak.

He frowned. 'Yeah, it was.'

She frowned then too. 'There's a problem with that?'

'Kisses like that feel like promises and I can't make you any of those, Princess.'

Can't or won't? Reality slammed back into place. She shook her hands free of his and snatched up a clean rag to clench them in. 'I told you there were a lot of reasons we shouldn't kiss.'

She backed up to lean against Candy's side, needing the support for knees that threatened to give way. 'I don't do short-term flings.'

He adjusted his stance and blew out a breath. 'Yet they're the only kind of relationships I have.'

'Strike One.'

She stared down at the rag, shut her eyes for a moment before lifting her chin and tossing back her hair. 'Everyone thinks I'm going to solve my current financial difficulties by finding a rich husband or boyfriend. You're rich. Strike Two.'

He slammed his hands to his hips. She opened her mouth to remind him about the grease and oil, but it was too late. His glare made her mouth dry. 'You're counting me out because I'm rich?'

She pushed upright from the van. 'I'm counting you out because you're rich *and* you can't commit. I'm not going to let you try to buy me off to salve a guilty conscience.'

His jaw clenched so hard she thought he might snap teeth. She pulled in a breath, held it for the count of three and released it.

'It's three strikes before I'm out. What's Strike Three?' he demanded.

She reached for, and found, her most supercilious shrug. 'What? Do you want me to do all of the hard work? Can't you possibly come up with a reason or ten of your own?' She made her voice deliberately scornful.

His eyes narrowed. Very slowly he sauntered to where she stood. Every instinct she had screamed for her to run. Except for those rogue ones that told her to grab him and kiss him again.

She squared her chin, forced herself to meet his gaze.

'You're confusing me with your lily-livered, pretty society boys, Princess. You won't get gallant manners from me. I'm debating the benefits of simply taking what I want—what, in fact, may be freely on offer—and to hell with the consequences.'

He slanted a deliberately insolent gaze down the length of her body and, to her horror, her nipples tightened and her thighs softened. How could he be so ruthless?

'Taking it and enjoying it…over and over—and, believe me, Princess, you'd enjoy it too—until I was sated.'

Her body responded to the smoky seduction of his voice.

'I know how to make a woman want…how to make her respond and to yield.'

She didn't doubt that for a moment.

'And what I want right now is you writhing beneath me, begging for release and calling my name as you come with the kind of orgasm that would blow your mind.'

Her breath caught and her stomach clenched. 'Why?' The word croaked out of her.

'The Princess submitting to the local bad-boy and begging for more—how satisfying would that be? What a triumph.'

She wanted him. His words set her body on fire. But they chilled her too. She didn't doubt that, if he put his mind to it, he could seduce her. She'd succumb. And it'd break her heart.

She met his gaze. 'If you do that, I will put you through as much hell as you do me. You might, in fact, be able to seduce me, but don't doubt for a moment that I have the ability to make you pay.'

They stared at each other for long fraught moments. He lifted his hand as if to touch the backs of his fingers to her cheek, but he stepped back with a low laugh and let his hand drop. 'We're not all that different after all, are we, Princess?'

'No.' But she didn't know if that were a strike against them or not.

They didn't speak again. Nell headed for the door of the garage. Rick turned back to Candy's engine. It didn't stop the burn in her body. It didn't stop the burn in her mind. It didn't stop the insane urge she had to throw herself face first onto the nearest available garden bench to cry.

She didn't. She just kept walking towards the house.

The money Rick promised arrived in her bank account the following Monday. Her bank manager rang to tell her the good news—and to try and pump her for information. She didn't tell him anything, but she frowned as she snapped her cellphone shut. Her father and the bank manager were still as thick as thieves. It'd mean her father would now hear about the upswing in her fortunes.

She should've taken the time and trouble to switch banks, but with everything else going on...

She shook the thought off. She'd deal with her father when she needed to and not before.

She and Rick were careful not to spend too much time in each other's company. He fixed Candy. He painted the drawing room and the library. She baked and delivered orders and went out in Candy—on Monday, Tuesday and Wednesday.

She waited till Thursday before approaching him. 'You haven't given me a contract to sign yet,' she reminded him.

'Do we really need something that formal?' He didn't look at her as he painted the library wall a soft, lush cream.

'Yes.'

'I'll get onto it.'

She made a sceptical, 'Hmph.' No doubt he'd get onto it the same way he'd got onto those receipts for building materials. She'd yet to see a single one.

The problem with Rick was that he had all of this money, but he simply didn't care about it. He probably wouldn't even notice if she paid him back or not. What he needed was a reason to care.

Her feet slowed. *Maybe...*

She came to a complete stop. *Well, why not?*

She made a beeline for the telephone to call her lawyer.

Rick started at the knock on his door on Friday evening. He glanced at his watch. It'd just gone six. *Who on earth...?*

Nell.

For a moment he was tempted to pretend he wasn't in.

Prison stole your courage.

With a muttered oath, he stormed over to the door and flung it open. Nell stood on the other side. Holding a bottle of champagne. Holy Mother of God! She wasn't going to try and seduce him, was she? Damn it, he wouldn't stand a chance and—

'Hello, Rick.'

It took all his strength not to shut the door in her face. 'What are you doing here, Nell?' He didn't have to work hard at making his voice unwelcoming. It came out that way. His only other option was to drag her into his arms and kiss her until neither one of them could think straight.

It'd taken all of his strength not to seduce her last week—every single ounce of it. He hadn't been able to recall anything he'd wanted more than to lose himself in her sweetness, to forget himself, to let himself believe in fairy tales if only for a few brief moments, to see if she could help heal the dark places inside him. He still wanted that with a fierceness that shocked him. And a man had only so much strength.

He hadn't seduced her then and he couldn't seduce her now. Nell deserved better from him. She deserved better from the world.

'Aren't you going to invite me in?'

'Do you think that wise?'

'I don't mean to stay long.'

He glanced at the champagne bottle and raised an eyebrow.

She laughed. 'I don't have shenanigans in mind. I just wanted to deliver this.' She held up an official-looking A4 business-size envelope.

Biting back a sigh, he moved to let her in, careful to keep his distance. 'What is it?'

She handed it to him. 'Open it and see.'

She sauntered across to the kitchen as if she owned the place. Which, technically speaking, she did. She reached up into the cupboard for two glasses. She didn't seem to mind that they were old food jars rather than champagne flutes. The cork of the champagne left the bottle with a pop. She didn't send it flying across the room, nor did she let a single drop of champagne fizz out of the bottle and onto the floor. She poured the bubbly, lifted both glasses and turned back to him.

'Well, open it.' She nodded at the envelope he still held. 'It's not an evil omen or bad news. I promise.'

God give him patience. He lifted the flap and slid out the single sheet of paper inside. He read it.

His heart stopped. The edges of his vision darkened. He blinked and read it again. His throat started to ache. She pushed one of the glasses into his hands, clinked it with hers and took a sip. He couldn't move.

'I wanted to say thank you, Rick.'

But...

'You've lent me the money that will allow me to follow my dream. I doubt there's anything I can do or say to tell you what that means to me. But I want you to know my gratitude is real, that I don't take your financial assistance for granted and that if, in the future, I can ever do you a good turn then I'll do my absolute best to deliver on that.'

He couldn't move and he couldn't speak. The ache in his throat travelled to his arms, his chest, his temples.

She set her glass on the tiny kitchen table, wiped her hands down the skirt of her Hawaiian frock. 'Well, that's all I wanted to say. I'll be off now. Enjoy your evening.'

'Nell…' He managed to croak out her name before she reached the door.

She turned.

'You've…you've…' She'd given him a thirty per cent share of her business! 'You can't do this.'

She frowned. 'Yes, I can.' Her frown deepened. 'Why not?'

'It's too much.'

Her face cleared. 'No, it's not. I talked it over with a lawyer. He assures me that's fair.'

'But I don't care about the money I'm lending you!'

She gave a little laugh, but there was more sadness in it than joy. 'I know, but I do. I care about it hugely. It means so much to me and I…I want to try and show you how much.'

She'd managed that, but…

'And I wanted…' her fingers clutched at the air

as if trying to find the words to explain '...I wanted to give you something back that might mean something to you. That's all.'

He rustled the paper entitling him to thirty per cent of her business under her nose. Was she crazy? 'You're giving me power over your dream!'

'Yes.'

She said that simply, as if it were no big thing, when it was the biggest thing he knew.

'I could destroy it!'

'Without you, my business had no chance of getting off the ground in the first place.'

'You shouldn't give anyone this kind of power over you.'

She moved forward and clasped his face in her hands and bizarrely it felt as if she held his heart instead. Those amazing green eyes blazed at him. 'I keep telling you that I trust you. Maybe now I've shown you how much.'

She pulled her hands away slowly, as if she'd have rather left them there. He stamped on the primal, savage impulses pounding through him. Impulses that ordered him to grab her and kiss her and to make her his.

She backed up a step as if she sensed the fight taking place inside him. Her eyes spoke of her own primal battle. He bit back a groan. She shot him a brave little smile. 'Enjoy the champagne.' And then she was gone.

Rick stumbled over to the sofa and collapsed onto

it. He knocked back a generous slug of champagne, coughing when the bubbles hit the back of his throat. He stared at the paper in his hands entitling him to thirty per cent of her business.

I trust you.

Thirty per cent!

Maybe now I've shown you how much.

Oh, she'd done that all right. Nobody had shown this much faith in him. Not ever. And he didn't know what to do with it. Just as he didn't know what to do with the conflicting emotions coursing through him—a mixture of dread and elation, fear and satisfaction.

Enjoy the champagne.

With a laugh, he took another sip. It was good stuff. The Princess didn't skimp at the big moments.

He paused halfway through his third sip. Maybe she had some ulterior motive, maybe…

His shoulders sank back into the softness of the sofa. She didn't have an ulterior motive. She wasn't playing some deep game. Nell had a heart as big as Sydney Harbour.

Something around his heart loosened then and some dark thing slipped away. Nell wanted to give him something important because she believed he deserved it, because she didn't believe he was a no-hoper or a loose cannon, but because she saw something in him that no one else saw.

And it gave him hope.

Not that he knew what he was hoping for.

* * *

The next morning—the thirteenth of March—Rick knocked on Nell's back door where before he'd have just strolled in. Before—as in before that kiss. His groin tightened at the memory.

Nell glanced over her shoulder and gestured him in. 'The paper's arrived.'

It sat on her table, still rolled up. She hadn't even had a peek, though he knew her curiosity must be eating her alive. She finished packing up a box of the most mouth-watering-looking cupcakes and set it on the end of the table with a host of other boxes. Pouring mugs of steaming hot coffee, she pushed one into his hand and sat at her usual spot at the table. She rolled the paper across to his usual spot.

A bad taste rose up in his mouth. He gulped coffee to chase it away. Nell stared at the paper and her nose curled. 'C'mon, then, there's no point in putting it off. We may as well find out what wild goose chase John means to send us on next.'

Us? He tried to resist the warmth the word threaded through him. 'Nell, you know you don't have to—'

'Yeah, right. Blah-blah fishcakes. You'd have never got this far without me, and you're not cutting me out of the game now.'

How was it this woman could make him grin at the most unlikely moments?

'And, look, I know it's not a game. I'm not trying to trivialise it.'

He knew that. He raised an eyebrow. 'Blah-blah fishcakes?'

'It's a wonderful phrase, don't you think? I mean to do my bit to bring it back into the common vernacular.'

She'd donned her prim and proper, hoity-toity princess manners, but he knew her well enough by now to know it for a sign of nerves.

'I'm not going to push you out of this, Princess. Rest easy. I just wanted to give you the chance to back out if that's what you'd prefer.'

She snorted in a very un-princess-like way. 'Get over yourself, tough guy. Sit. Turn to the classifieds.'

She was right. Putting it off was pointless. With a sigh, he did as she bid.

He pushed his coffee to one side. He didn't want it. He'd had one earlier. The Princess drank far too much of the stuff. He opened his mouth, only to shut it again. Now mightn't be the time for that particular lecture. Instead, he ran his fingers down the line of classifieds. On a Saturday morning the paper was full of birthday and anniversary announcements, of births, deaths and marriages, and personal ads.

His finger stopped. '*Rick*,' he read.

'What is it?' Nell demanded.

'*Freemont Park. Two p.m. Wear your party clothes.*'

'What on earth…?' She leapt out of her chair and came to stand behind him to read over his shoulder, her hand resting lightly against his back. His heart rate kicked up at the warm feel of her. She read John's message, harrumphed and went back to sit in her chair. Rick closed his eyes and pulled in a breath. 'He's proving just as chatty in death as he was in life.'

Rick laughed. Nell flipped open her laptop. 'Okay, Freemont Park. It's in the south-eastern suburbs. It'll take us the best part of forty minutes to get there.'

Rick thrust out his jaw. 'I'm not wearing party clothes.'

Nell leapt to her feet. 'I'm off to do my deliveries. I'll meet you in the garage at one o'clock sharp. Right?'

He scowled. 'Right.'

Nell and Rick stood on the edge of the park and glanced around at the assorted picnickers and walkers.

'Where in the hell are we supposed to start?'

Rick's face had gone as tight as his shoulders. She clutched a box of cupcakes and pulled air into her lungs. 'It's not a ridiculously large park.'

'It's big enough!'

'We'll just amble for a while.'

She hooked her hand through his elbow and propelled them forward, setting them on a path that led diagonally through the park. They must look an odd couple. She wore her cherry print dress with a red patent leather belt and heels. Rick wore his oldest jeans—torn at the knee—and a tight black T-shirt. He hadn't shaved.

In defiance of John's strictures?

She didn't mind. That T-shirt showed off the breadth of his shoulders to perfection and did rather nice things for his biceps. If he'd stop scowling at their surroundings he'd be downright hot and handsome.

Oh, who was she kidding? He was devastatingly and dangerously delicious, regardless of what expression he wore. And that day-old growth…

She had a vision of being stretched out beside him and running her tongue across his jaw and…

'Any particular reason you're pinching me, Princess?'

Oh! She relaxed her grip and swallowed. 'Sorry.'

She forced her gaze and mind from Rick's, uh, finer points, to focus on their surroundings until her breathing returned to within the realms of normal. The park was lush and green, with distant views of the harbour. Gum trees and Norfolk Island pines swayed in the breeze, providing shade for picnic blankets and camp chairs. Oleanders in lush blooms of pink, white and red added a riot of colour. At one end stood a rotunda amid a rose garden.

The bright sunshine, blue sky and chatter from a flock of nearby rainbow lorikeets spoke of summer, holiday fun and relaxation and something inside her yearned towards it all.

A rowdy and boisterous happy birthday chorus

had them both turning to their right. They moved off the path and onto the grass, stopping by an oleander in full pink flower to watch.

'Happy birthday, dear Poppy...'

She couldn't help smiling. There had to be a crowd of at least twenty people—of varying ages—and everyone was smiling and jolly. An ache started up inside her chest. 'I always wanted a family like this,' she whispered. People who loved each other—enjoyed each other's company—and wanted to spend time together.

'Me too.'

Of course he had. She had no right to moan when one compared her childhood to his.

They continued to watch. Small children danced around, elderly folk sat in chairs, and everyone else stood as they hip-hip-hoorayed. What must it be like to be the focus of all that love? The birthday girl cut the cake, but her back was mostly to them. She mightn't be able to see it, but Nell could imagine the breadth of the girl's smile.

Oh, if only this could be Rick's new family!

'Poppy is a botanical name,' she offered.

'Grasping at straws, aren't you?'

Probably. With a shrug, she turned back to survey the party. And then the birthday girl swung around and Nell's breath jammed in her throat.

Oh, my God!

Oh! My! God!

When she was able to tear her gaze away she

glanced up at Rick. Had he seen it? The family resemblance was unmistakable.

Rick's eyes had fixed on the girl's face. His jaw clenched tight and his chest rose and fell as if he'd been running. 'How old do you think she is?'

The words growled out of him and Nell had to swallow before she could speak. 'Eighteen or nineteen.' She had no idea what to do.

A woman, probably in her late forties, turned at that moment and saw them. With a smile, she set off towards them. With a curse, Rick turned and strode away, his long legs eating up the distance.

'Oh, Rick, wait! I—'

'Hello?'

Nell turned and hoped her smile didn't appear as sick and green as she felt. 'Um, hello. I… Well, we…I…kind of received an invitation.' It wasn't precisely a lie.

'You must be one of Poppy's friends. I'm her mother, Marigold Somers.'

Marigold! She reached out to steady herself against the oleander.

'Is everything okay with your friend?'

Oh, dear Lord. 'He…he had to take an urgent phone call.'

'Never mind, come and join the party.'

'Oh, I don't think I can.'

The woman stared at her.

Um...what to do? 'You see, my invitation came from a rather unusual source and…' She bit her lip.

'My name is Nell Smythe-Whittaker and I don't know Poppy, but I believe you knew my late gardener and...'

The woman blanched. 'Oh, please, no!'

The distress in Marigold's face tore at her. She reached out to clasp the other woman's hand. 'Oh, please, I haven't come to cause you any trouble, but...'

'But?'

'Did you know John died?'

She swallowed and nodded. 'Yes.'

'Did you know he left behind another child?'

Her jaw slackened. 'You?'

'Not me.'

'Your friend?'

'I...'

Others in the group were starting to glance in their direction. Nell didn't want to create a scene. It wasn't her scene to create. She wanted to find Rick. That was what she really wanted to do. She pushed the box of cupcakes into Marigold's hands. 'Say they're from a secret admirer. My card is taped to the lid. Please call me?'

The other woman nodded and, before anyone else from the party could approach, Nell turned and made her way back the way she'd come—as quickly as she could on grass in heels.

So...

They'd found Rick's sibling. Finally. She didn't blame him for his shock, but... *Oh, my word.* To be a part of such a family! Her heart pounded against her ribcage, the blood raced through her veins. Still, there were so many variables. Did Poppy know she was John's child? And how would she react to discovering she had a brother?

And, of course, there was Rick.

He was waiting for her in the car. She slid into the passenger seat, turned to him and opened her mouth.

'Don't.'

She winced at the darkness in his eyes.

'Put your seat belt on.'

Once she had he pulled the car onto the road and roared away from the park. She glanced once more at him before keeping her eyes fixed to the front. Swallowing, she tried to put herself in his shoes. It had to be a shock to come face to face with someone who looked so much like you.

The shock she understood, but the anger...?

After a moment she shook her head. No, she understood that too and Rick was entitled to it. How dared John and Marigold keep such secrets? How dared John taunt Rick with a vision of a life that had been closed to him his entire childhood?

And how dared John father children he'd had no intention of nurturing!

When they arrived home, Nell leapt out of the car to open the gate to the garage. Rick drove in, just as silent as he'd been for the entire trip back.

She folded her arms and leant against the doorway as he emerged from the car.

He barely met her gaze. 'I'm leaving. Today.'

What the...? She didn't move. 'The hell you are.'

He swung to her with a glare that should've reduced her to ash, but she rushed on before he could blast her with a barrage of abuse. 'You promised me until the end of next week. We signed an agreement. You *will* keep your word.'

He stabbed a finger at her. 'That agreement is not some binding contract! And—'

'Regardless of any of this other nonsense, you owe me.'

'I owe you nothing!'

She agreed with that but had no intention of telling him so. 'I've kept my word to you. In fact, I've more than kept it. You can jolly well do the same.'

'What the hell for?' he shouted at her.

She gripped her hands in front of her. 'Because we're friends and that's what friends do.'

He stilled

'And because none of this situation is of my making.'

He dragged a hand down his face. 'You're right. You don't deserve this from me.'

'The situation isn't of your making either, Rick. You're entitled to your anger.'

He fixed her with that hard gaze. He stalked over to her, intent outlined in every muscle. 'You promise me right now that you won't interfere any further in this godforsaken mess.'

'What are you going to do about this godforsaken mess?'

'Nothing.'

Her jaw dropped.

'That girl's life is perfect.'

'You can't know that after five minutes of spying from the bushes!'

'And she sure as hell doesn't need someone like me coming in and ruining things.'

'Ruining?' Her jaw worked. 'You're her *brother*.'

'We're strangers.' He fixed her with a glare. 'And you either butt out or I leave now.'

She held up her hands. 'Fine, whatever.' But if he thought this situation had finished playing out he was seriously mistaken.

'And, Nell, I will be leaving at the end of next week.'

She didn't bother trying to disguise the way her face fell. 'I'm sorry about that. I'll miss you, Rick.'

He froze for a moment, closed his eyes and dragged a hand down his face. Nell turned and left. She didn't wait to hear what sop he meant to throw her. It wouldn't help to soften the blow.

Blinking hard, she made her way across the garden…to find the kitchen door open. She had locked it, hadn't she?

She went to call for Rick when a figure appeared in the doorway. 'Good afternoon, Nell.'

Her heart slithered to its knees. She forced her legs forward. 'Hello, Father.'

CHAPTER TEN

NELL MADE COFFEE out of habit. She set a mug in front of her father. She was too tired for games. 'I expect this isn't a social call?'

'I want the money you made from pawning your grandmother's diamond ring.'

It took all of her strength not to throw her coffee at him. She pulled in a breath, held it and then slowly let it out. 'I know you already pawned it and replaced it with a copy, a fake. Why are you playing this game with me?'

He leapt out of his chair so fast it fell to the floor, his face twisting in purple fury. 'It's a what?'

She stilled. For a moment she almost believed him and then she remembered what he was like. 'You're afraid I'll go to the police and that the theft of the jewels will be traced back to you.'

'Those jewels should've been mine!'

'But they were left to me. What a scandal it'd be if it was known you'd hocked your mother's jewels— jewels that rightfully belonged to your daughter. It'd serve you right if I did go to the police.'

He stared at her. Very slowly the ugly colour faded from his cheeks, replaced with a calculating gleam in his eyes that was twice as ugly and had acid burning in her stomach.

She set her coffee down, folded her arms and leaned back against the sink. 'Who told you I'd found the ring?'

'I know you found more than just the ring.'

It took an effort not to sneer. 'I'm getting a new bank manager.'

'I know who you have living here.'

'What business is it of yours?'

'Rick Bradford's a thief, a drug addict and a jail-bird.'

Her composure vaporised. Coffee sloshed over the sides of her mug. 'He's a hundred times the man you are!'

He laughed. He actually laughed. He righted his chair, sat and sipped his coffee. 'Daughter, here's how it's going to be. You're putting this house on the market.'

It was her turn to laugh. Oh, this should be good. 'How do you propose to convince me of that?'

'If you don't, I'm going to lodge a complaint with the police. I'm going to tell them your grandmother's jewels were stolen and replaced with copies and where do you think suspicion will fall?'

'You!'

'I'll make sure it falls on your little friend, Rick Bradford.'

Her heart flew up into her throat. She fought for breath. 'It'll never stick. He's innocent!'

He laughed again, and too late she realised her mistake. She'd shown weakness, had bared her Achilles heel.

'I know when he started living here. I know when you placed those jewels in the safety deposit box. I know he had the opportunity.'

No!

'And, given his background, he'd have had the means.'

Rick was innocent!

'He'll be hauled in for questioning. I will bribe men to say he took the rings to them for copies to be made. I will make sure he goes down for it.'

Her heart pounded. She couldn't speak. Would her father really stoop so low? He knew people. He still had connections, but would he really...?

He shook his head, his eyes hard. 'I wasn't born to be a poor man, Nell, and I have no intention of remaining poor. The sale of this house will get me out of trouble and give me a chance to rebuild my business.'

'And you really don't care who you hurt in the process?'

'It's a dog eat dog world.'

'You really don't care that if you do this I will disown you? That I will never speak to you again?'

He laughed. It was an ugly sound that made her stomach churn. 'You'll come crawling back when you see the money come rolling in, demanding your share. Just like your mother. Yes, you're your mother's daughter. Mind you, I'll be generous.'

She stared at him. Had she ever really known him? 'What a sad life you must have.'

He stiffened.

'You judge your value by the amount of money you have rather than anything more substantial like how good you are at certain things or the good you do or the friends you have. I…I wouldn't want to be like you for all the jewels in Grandma's jewellery box.'

'Excellent.' He rose. 'Then you won't mind handing them over when I return tomorrow with the estate agent. There'll be a sale contract for you to sign.'

Her heart pounded. Sell the house? The house counted for nothing beside Rick's freedom, but… *Oh, Grandma, I'm sorry.*

'You can make all the pretty little moral speeches you want, daughter…'

He said that word as if he owned her. Her chin snapped up. He didn't own her. Nobody owned her. She was her own woman.

'But I don't see you making a success of yourself from whatever it is you're good at. I don't see you doing any good in the world. I don't see you surrounded by loving and loyal friends.'

She forced herself to meet his gaze. 'Maybe not, but I'm a hundred times the person you are.' And she knew that now, deep down in her bones. 'At least I can sleep at night.'

He blinked.

'You might regain your riches, but you're going to be a very lonely man if you insist on this course.' She gestured to the house. 'If you have any feeling for me whatsoever turn back now and there may still be a chance we could forge some kind of relationship. If you don't…' she pulled in a breath, all the while maintaining eye contact with him '…when I marry, you won't be invited to my wedding. When I have children, you will not be allowed to meet them. And don't bother calling for me when you're on your deathbed because I will not come.'

His gaze hardened. 'You always were a stupid and useless girl.'

The old taunt had her shoulders inching up to her ears. She forced them back down. She wasn't useless.

'I'll bring the estate agent around at eleven on the dot. Be here.'

'It's a Sunday!'

The smile he sent her was pure smug self-satisfaction. 'There are buyers interested, and some people who still jump when I ask it of them.'

Unlike an ungrateful, useless daughter?

He left. Nell limped over to a chair and lowered herself into it. If she didn't do as he ordered, he would send Rick to prison. She didn't doubt his ruthlessness…or how much he wanted the money the sale of Whittaker House would bring. And it wasn't just ruthlessness, but spite. Spite directed at her for not jumping when he demanded it, for not marrying money when he'd ordered it, for not getting him out of his financial straits.

Signing over her apartment and sports car and her trust fund—none of that counted as far as he was concerned. Apparently she was still useless!

She ground her teeth together. She wasn't useless. In fact, that had been a darn fine ultimatum she'd given him. And she'd meant it. Every word. Not that it had done any good. She swallowed, battling nausea. She rubbed her temples. What guarantee did she have that her father wouldn't go after Rick once the house was sold anyway, just to punish her? She might not be useless, but she needed advice.

But who could she turn to?

She tapped her fingers against the wooden table top. Who wouldn't go tattling to her father the minute her back was turned—the sleazy solicitor? Not likely.

The thing was, her father had been right on that head. She wasn't surrounded by an army of loving and loyal friends. She had one friend in the world—Rick—and she wasn't telling him about this. She wasn't giving him the chance to be noble. She didn't need noble.

One friend… She pushed a hand back through her hair. *Useless…*

A moment later she straightened. She mightn't have any friends, but Rick did.

She reached for the phone book, searched and then punched a number into the phone. 'Tash? Hello, it's Nell Smythe-Whittaker. I was wondering if I could possibly trouble Mr King—uh, Mitch—for a quick word?'

'He's not here at the moment. Would you like me to have him drop by some time?'

'Oh, no, not here.' She didn't want Rick to see.

'Would you like to make an appointment at the station?'

'God, no!'

Tash didn't say anything for a moment. 'Nell, are you in some kind of trouble?'

'I…I don't know. And please don't mention this to Rick. I don't need a white knight—I just need some advice.'

'Okay.'

But she drew the word out and Nell knew Tash would talk to Rick eventually. Her loyalty did reside with him, after all.

She swallowed. 'Would it be possible…I mean would you mind if I came over to your place at a time convenient to both you and Mitch?'

'Sure, why not? Mitch should be here within the next half an hour if you're free this afternoon.'

'Thanks, Tash.'

She knew the other woman didn't think much of

her, and she didn't blame her. But at that moment she could've hugged her.

Nell sat opposite Tash and Mitch at Tash's kitchen table and her mouth went dry. What if they accused her of ruining Rick's life? She'd have no answer for that.

'Would you like me to leave the two of you alone?' Tash eventually said.

Nell shook her head. Tash should know what was in the works in case Rick needed her. Besides, it didn't take a genius to work out that Tash and Mitch were besotted with each other. And not just besotted but a team. If Tash left now, Mitch would only fill her in later.

She was the outsider here. And as long as she made sure nothing bad happened to Rick because of her father then it didn't much matter what either Tash or Mitch thought of her.

She lifted her chin. 'I guess I better start at the very beginning so you get the full picture.'

'Sounds like a plan.' Mitch nodded his encouragement and his calm sense helped ease the racing of her pulse and frightened leaps of her heart. She could see why Tash had fallen for him.

She told them how she and Rick had searched John's cottage. She didn't tell them about John's letter, though. That was Rick's secret to tell. She told them about finding the jewellery box and how she'd asked Rick to put it back, thinking it'd be safe there.

She told them about the deal she and Rick had come to—rent-free accommodation in return for maintenance work on Whittaker House—and how after one night in the cottage he'd refused to keep the jewels there and how she'd put them in a safety deposit box at the bank.

As she spoke, Tash's face grew darker. Mitch merely listened, his eyes intent, his face revealing nothing of his thoughts.

And then she told them about her father's threats and demands. Tash's face darkened further. She leaned across the table towards Nell, but Nell held up a hand. 'I know, okay, I know. My father is a nasty piece of work. I'll do what he demands…I'll sell my grandmother's house.' Her voice cracked. She swallowed and cleared her throat. 'But none of that will ensure Rick's safety. I mean, once the house is sold and my father has the money, what's to stop him from attempting to press charges against Rick anyway?'

Hell, if her father found out how much money Rick had… The thought made her temples throb.

Tash slumped back. 'You believe Rick is innocent then?'

'Of course he's innocent!' Surely Tash hadn't thought—

'Who do you think is responsible?' Mitch broke in.

'My father, of course.'

Mitch frowned. 'But you said he demanded the money you made from the sale of the ring.'

'No doubt to cover his tracks. He has no right to that jewellery. It was left to me. I could press charges against him if I chose to.' Not that she would.

'The rest of the jewellery is still in the bank?'

'Yes.' First thing on Monday she was changing banks.

'Would you trust me with it?'

She gazed at Mitch. 'Of course I would, but, Mitch, I don't want to make any of this official.'

Tash straightened. 'What do you want?'

'I want to ensure Rick is free from any of this. I want to make sure my father can't go after him.'

Mitch nodded. 'You said you're signing a contract with some estate agent tomorrow?'

'Yes.' She could barely get the word out.

'You're not doing that on your own. I'm sending my solicitor along.'

'I'll pay.'

Tash shook her head. 'We'll sort all of that out later.'

Nell swallowed and fished the diamond ring—the fake diamond ring—from her pocket and set it in front of Mitch. 'I'll retrieve the rest of the jewellery first thing Monday—I expect they'll all be fakes.'

Mitch surveyed the ring. 'Whittaker House is in your name, right? That means, even if a buyer is found immediately, we have six weeks before the property officially changes hands and the bulk of the money is transferred into your account.'

Which she'd then have to transfer to her father.

'That means for at least the next six weeks, Rick is safe.'

A sigh eased out of her. Six weeks of knowing Rick couldn't be hauled in and charged with a crime he hadn't committed. But what then…? All the tension shot back into her.

'If we have to,' Mitch said, 'we'll force your father to sign a clause to the effect that he won't press charges against Rick.'

That could be done? Nell sagged in relief. 'Thank you.'

There didn't seem to be anything else to say after that, so Nell left.

'Damn!' Tash muttered as she and Mitch watched Nell drive away.

Mitch rested an arm across her shoulders. 'What?'

'She's in love with him.'

'Lucky man.'

Tash snorted. 'As soon as he realises he'll bolt.'

'Why?'

She shook her head. 'He just will. It's what he does.'

'She's prepared to make a hell of a sacrifice for him.'

Tash glanced up. 'Will we be able to get him off the hook *and* save her house?'

'We'll give it our best shot.'

She reached up on her tiptoes to kiss him. 'Have I mentioned lately how much I love you?'

Nell wasn't sure what to do when she returned home. Start packing boxes in preparation for her imminent eviction?

She fell into a chair, pulled a box of cupcakes towards her, opened the lid, stared at them for a few moments before pushing them away again. Eating cupcakes wouldn't make her feel better.

She could hear Rick hammering something in the dining room, even though it was past six o'clock on a Saturday evening. She should tell him not to bother. She should tell him…

She dropped her head to the table. How was she going to explain selling Whittaker House to him? She'd have to give him his money back too, of course. The dream of a Victorian teahouse wasn't going to come to fruition any time soon.

She frowned. Had her bank manager traced where that money had come from? If so, had he informed her father? She lifted her head…

To find herself staring at a woman in the doorway. *Marigold.*

Marigold shifted her weight from one foot to the other. 'Have I come at a bad time?'

Nell stared and then shot to her feet. 'Of course not. I… Please! Come in.'

She thought about Rick thumping away in the

dining room and swallowed. Dear Lord, all of this could end in tears. Lcts of tears.

Mostly hers, probably.

She swallowed, but the uncertainty in the other woman's face caught at her. 'Please, sit down. Can I get you a coffee or a soda?'

Marigold perched on a chair, twisting her hands together, her eyes wide in a pale face and Nell shrugged—nothing practised or elegant, but simply a shrug. 'To heck with that, let's have some wine.'

She pulled a bottle from the fridge, grabbed two glasses and poured. 'You'll have to excuse this—' she handed Marigold a glass '—but it's cheap and cheerful rather than elegant and expensive.'

'If it's alcohol, bring it on.'

'Amen, sister.'

They clinked and drank. Rather deeply. Nell topped up the glasses and then wondered what to do…what to say.

'I remember when you were a little girl.'

Nell's glass halted halfway to her mouth. 'You do?'

'I went to school with your mother. I came to a few parties and afternoon teas here over the years. You'd have not been more than six or seven when I fell pregnant with Poppy.'

'And that's when you stopped coming round?'

Marigold took a gulp of her wine and nodded. 'I met John at one of those parties.'

'And you had an affair?'

Marigold stared down into her wine and a tiny smile touched her lips. 'We did, yes. It was rather short-lived, but intense. We were very careful to keep it secret. If we'd been discovered John would've lost his job and my friends would've…well, they wouldn't have understood.'

Wow! 'And you fell pregnant?'

She nodded and they both gulped wine. 'That's when things turned bad. John wanted nothing to do with a baby.'

Nell swallowed. *Double wow.* 'Do you know why?'

'Not really. I glimpsed something extraordinary in him, but there was a hardness there too. Maybe it's because he grew up in a boys' home and from what I understand it was a rather brutal place. He never said as much, but I don't believe he trusted himself around children. Or maybe he didn't want to be reminded of the childhood he'd had.'

'Does Poppy know he was her father?'

Marigold nodded. 'I told her when she turned fifteen. You see, she knew the man who she calls Dad—my husband Neville, who she adores and who adores her back—wasn't her biological father; we met when she was two. But she really wanted to know who her biological father was…and it only seemed fair to tell her.

'She sent him a letter that he never answered, and she insisted on sending him an invitation to her birthday party every year—the party in the park is an annual tradition. But he never did turn up.'

Nell stared into her glass of cheap wine and recalled the way he hadn't let her plant marigolds. Was it because they'd have reminded him of this woman and a vision of a different life, a different path he could've taken? None of them would ever know now.

A sigh escaped the other woman. 'But if Poppy has a brother…'

Nell glanced up.

'Well, of course, she has every right to know him. I can't prevent that and I wouldn't want to. All I ask is that you give me a chance to tell her about him first, that's all.'

'But of course!'

'I'm sorry I panicked earlier and—'

'Nell!'

Rick's voice boomed down the hallway, his footsteps growing louder. 'Where the hell have you put the masking tape?'

He stopped dead in the doorway. Across the table from her, Marigold gasped. 'Dear heaven, you're the spitting image.'

Those dark eyes fixed on Nell with an accusation that cut her to her very marrow. Very softly he said, 'Deal's off.' He walked through the kitchen, out of the back door, and she knew he headed for John's cottage to pack. To leave. For good.

'What just happened?' Marigold whispered.

Nell blinked hard. She reached for her wine and

tried to force a sip past the lump in her throat. 'Rick is… I don't think he means to make himself known to Poppy. He thinks it'll complicate her life.' *And he thinks I betrayed him.*

Marigold rose. 'I mean to tell Poppy about him. She has a right to know and I don't want there to be any lies between us.'

Nell rose too. Marigold pushed a card into her hands. 'I sincerely hope you can convince that young man to reconsider his decision. Perhaps you'll be kind enough to give him this?'

Nell stared down at the card—a business card with Marigold's phone number and address. 'Yes, of course.'

Marigold left. Nell grabbed her glass of wine and drained it. Then she headed outside for the cottage. She knocked twice—a quick rat-tat—and then opened the door and walked in.

Rick whirled around from throwing things into a holdall. 'I didn't say you could come in,' he snarled.

'Oh, for heaven's sake, shut up and listen for once, will you?'

He glared. She merely thrust her chin up a little higher. 'You need to know some things.'

'If it's anything to do with Poppy or John-bloody-Cox then no, I don't.'

'Back at the park after you raced off,' she said as if he hadn't spoken, 'I told Marigold that John Cox had another child.'

'You had no right!'

She snapped herself to her full height. 'If you'd hung around I'd have let you deal with it, but you'd raced off! You left me to improvise the best I could.'

His glare didn't lower by a single degree.

'Marigold—that's Poppy's mother—went pale at the news. So I pushed the box of cupcakes at her, told her my business card was taped to the lid and asked her to contact me. And then I left. That's what happened in the park and that's why Marigold was in the kitchen this afternoon. She didn't ring or give me any warning.'

'You were drinking wine together!'

'I wasn't going to turn her away! Besides, she was nervous...and so was I. Wine seemed like a good idea.' She thrust her chin out, daring him to challenge her. 'And it still does.'

Rick dragged a hand down his face.

'And now you can jolly well listen to what she had to say.' And then she outlined the conversation she and Marigold had just shared, leaving nothing out.

'I don't care,' he said when she finished.

Her heart stuttered. 'But—'

'I'm leaving.'

Just as she'd known he would, but it didn't stop the blow from nearly cutting her in half. Given her father's threats, it'd probably be better if he did leave. If he left Sydney and went far, far away, but...

But it didn't mean he had to turn his back on his family!

'Do whatever you damn well please!' she hollered at him. She strode forward to poke him in the shoulder. 'We can't choose our families. You and me, we're perfect proof of that except…'

She whirled away from him. 'Except in this case you can choose—you can decide to choose your sister!' She swung back. His face had gone pale and wooden. 'Poppy seems lovely. Marigold seems lovely. Her husband Neville sounds lovely. They all seem lovely, but you're not going to choose them— you're going to reject them instead. Just like John did!'

Rick's jaw worked for a moment, but no words came out. 'Reject?' he finally spat out. 'Their lives are perfect!' He wasn't going to waltz in there and ruin it for them.

He'd met people like that before—good, decent people who wouldn't turn him away. But their lives would be that bit worse for knowing him, their happiness diminished. They didn't deserve that. That lovely girl—his sister! She didn't deserve that.

Nell glared at him. 'Who's to say their lives wouldn't be more perfect with you in it?'

He stepped in close to her, pushed his face close to hers and tried to ignore the sweet scent of cake and sugar and spice. 'Fairy tales don't come true.'

'You have a sister. *That's* a reality. This *isn't* a fairy tale.'

Her belief in happy ever afters was a fiction, though, and he had to take a step back before some of that magic took hold of him. 'This is my decision to make.'

Her head snapped up. 'You're going to walk away?'

He glanced heavenward. 'Finally she gets the message.'

'Fine!'

He glanced back down.

'Marigold asked me to give you this.' She took his hand and slapped a business card into it and then dropped his hand as if she couldn't bear to touch him. 'Now get the hell off my property.'

Rick scowled and pounded on Tash's door. Tash opened it. 'Is it okay if I bunk here tonight?' he asked without preamble.

'Sure.' She pushed the door wide. 'I take it you and Nell have had words.'

'What?' He rounded on her.

Tash didn't even blink at his growl. She gestured for him to dump his stuff in the spare bedroom and then continued through to the living room. Mitch sat at the table. He and Rick nodded their greetings to each other. Tash turned. 'You ought to know she was here earlier.'

He slammed his hands to his hips 'So she told you about John Cox and Poppy and the whole mess of it, I suppose, and tried to enlist your help?'

Mitch opened his mouth but Tash took the seat

beside him, elbowing him in the ribs, and he shut it again. 'Something like that. She made a good case.'

'Can it, Tash.' He couldn't believe she'd be on Nell's side. 'I don't care if that girl is my sister.' And it didn't matter what Nell or Tash or Mitch had to say about the matter. 'There's no law that says I have to meet her.'

'Holy crap!' Tash's jaw dropped. 'John Cox, the gardener, is your father?'

He stilled and then swore. She'd played him to perfection. If Nell hadn't riled him up so much he'd have never fallen for one of Tash's tricks.

'*And* he fathered more than one child?'

He closed his eyes.

'That wasn't the mess she told us about.'

Obviously. He waited for Tash to grill him further, but she didn't. A wave of affection washed over him then. Tash knew how to give a guy the space and privacy he needed. His face darkened. Unlike some others he could name. He glanced up, but the expression on Tash's face made his blood chill. He straightened. 'What the hell was she here for then?'

Tash and Mitch shared a glance. 'You might want to sit down to hear this, Rick,' Mitch said.

CHAPTER ELEVEN

RICK LISTENED TO the tale Tash and Mitch recounted with growing disbelief. 'You have to be joking? You're telling me she's going to sell her house—the house she's done everything in her power to hang onto—in an attempt to keep me out of jail?'

'That's exactly what we're saying.'

Oh, Princess. 'She knows that's crazy, right?'

'No,' Tash said, as if it were obvious it wasn't crazy. Or as if it should've been obvious to him that Nell wouldn't think it crazy. She had a point.

'And she'd be right,' Mitch said. 'It's not crazy.'

Ice filtered through his gut. He wasn't going to prison again for anyone. Ever. Again.

Except...

Except he wasn't letting the Princess sell out on his behalf.

'She picked a fight with me on purpose. She kicked me out to get me out of the way.' Because Nell could twist him around her little finger and if she'd wanted him to stay, if she'd argued with him to stay, if she'd promised no more interference on the Poppy and Marigold front, he'd have stayed.

'That's my best guess,' Tash said. 'It's what I'd have done in her shoes.'

Rick's mouth opened but no words came out.

'She has a point, Rick. It might be best if you do disappear.'

And leave Nell to bumble along as best she could? 'No way, I'm not going anywhere.'

Tash fixed him with a look that made him fidget. He rolled his shoulders. 'I'll buy the bloody house.'

'No you won't!'

Tash and Mitch both said that at the same time. He scowled at them. Mitch leaned towards him. 'It wouldn't be a good idea at this point in time for Roland Smythe-Whittaker to know you have money.'

Rick slumped back in his chair, silently acknowledging the truth of that.

Mitch glanced at his watch. 'I've gotta go.' He rose, kissed Tash and left.

'Do you have enough money to buy Whittaker House?'

He nodded.

'How?'

He lifted a shoulder. 'It's amazing how much money you can make playing poker, Tash.'

She closed her eyes. 'Oh, Rick.'

He didn't know why, but her words burned through him. He shifted on his chair. 'I could buy the house anonymously.'

Tash grabbed two beers from the fridge and tossed him one. 'No.'

His hand tightened around the can. 'This is not your decision to make!'

She snorted at him. 'What would you be doing tomorrow if we hadn't told you about the situation?'

He didn't answer.

'You'd jump in your car and head up the coast without a backward glance, right?'

She was spot on. As usual. The thing was, she had told him about the mess Nell was in and—

'She came to us for help—me and Mitch—not you. It's not even help but advice she asked for. All Mitch and I plan to do is arm her with the information she needs to make her next move.'

He opened his mouth, but she cut him off. 'She said she doesn't want some white knight riding in and saving the day.' Tash took a long slug of her beer. 'She's not some helpless woman you can ride in and rescue to ease your damn guilt, Rick.'

'What guilt?'

'The guilt at leaving.'

He stared at her. He could barely breathe, let alone speak.

'She can save herself. What's more, I think she needs to do this on her own so she can prove exactly that.'

The Princess was resilient—strong. It was just...

He wanted to be her white knight.

Why? To ease his guilt, as Tash said? His stomach churned. 'She thinks you don't like her, you know?' It would've taken a lot of courage for her to approach Tash.

'I don't really know her, but I like her just fine. I *really* like what she's prepared to do for you.'

That only made his stomach churn harder. 'It harks back to when you made it clear she should leave the Royal Oak after one drink and kept such a close eye on her the entire time.'

Tash stared at her beer. 'I didn't want any trouble. I didn't want anyone hassling her. Her father wasn't a popular man at the time.'

'I knew it'd be something like that.'

'She's in love with you, Rick.'

His beer halted halfway to his mouth. His heart pounded.

'Don't play games with her.'

He wanted to jump up and run.

'You have two choices as far as I can see. You either get up in the morning, get in your car and drive off into the sunset.'

He thrust out his jaw. He wasn't leaving. Not until he knew Nell and her dreams were safe.

'Or if you're so hell-bent on sticking around you better start doing something to deserve her.'

Tash rose then and left the room. He realised his beer was still stranded at that crazy angle and he lowered it to the table, his heart pounding. Why wasn't he already in his car, tearing away from Sydney as if the hounds of hell were at his heels?

Because Nell was about to sacrifice everything that most mattered to her for him.

For him!

He couldn't let her do that, because…

He stared at the wall opposite as it all fell into place. He loved Nell. He was in love with the Princess.

Somewhere along the line her dreams had become his dreams. She'd given meaning to his hobo existence and he didn't want to go back to drifting aimlessly through life.

He wanted…

He swallowed and tapped a finger against his beer. He wanted the dream he'd had before he'd gone to prison. He wanted the wife and kids and a regular job. He wanted a place in the world and he wanted that place right by Nell's side.

You better start doing something to deserve her.

On Sunday her father and Byron Withers, the estate agent, arrived promptly at eleven a.m.

Byron smirked at her with so much I-told-you-so satisfaction it was all Nell could do not to seize him by the ear and toss him back out of the front door. It took an effort to pull all of her haughty superiority around her, but she did. She wasn't giving these two men the satisfaction of knowing how much she cried inside.

Besides, she was doing this for Rick. He didn't

deserve what her father had planned for him and that gave her strength too.

Both men, though, faltered when they found the solicitor Mitch had organised for her already ensconced at the kitchen table.

'This isn't necessary,' her father boomed.

'Nevertheless, I am having Mr Browne read over the contract before I sign it. That's non-negotiable.' She wasn't afraid her father would walk away in a huff. She knew how much he wanted the sale of Whittaker House to go through. 'So the sooner Mr Withers hands the contract over the sooner my solicitor can read it and the sooner you can both be on your way.'

With a curt nod from her father, Byron Withers did as she'd suggested. She'd provided Mr Browne with coffee and cupcakes when he'd arrived. Her father eyed the cupcakes hungrily. 'Coffee, daughter?'

'No, Roland, I'm afraid there's none on offer.' She'd never called him by his Christian name before and the shock in his eyes gave her little pleasure. But she wanted him to know that she'd meant what she'd said to him the previous day. If he insisted she sell Whittaker House, if he persisted in his threats against Rick, she would never acknowledge him as her father again.

The solicitor glanced up. 'We are not signing this clause, this clause or this clause. Mr Withers, these are not only immoral but they're bordering on illegal.'

Her father's cheeks reddened and his face darkened.

The solicitor turned to her. 'If it's okay with you, I'd like to take this to the authority that is, in effect, the Estate Agents' watchdog. This kind of thing shouldn't be allowed.'

Thank you, Mitch.

Byron came bustling up between them. 'I'm sure there's no need for that! It'll have merely been some innocent oversight by the contract department.'

'But—' Her father broke off at Byron's shake of his head. He took to glowering at her instead.

She folded her arms and glared back while her solicitor forced Byron to initial the changes and insert clauses that had apparently gone inadvertently 'missing'. 'I've had a lifetime of that look,' she informed him. 'But I find I'm impervious to it now.'

His jaw dropped.

They both glanced back to the table when Byron groaned. 'But that means she can pull out of the sale at any time without making any financial recompense to the agency for advertising or…or…anything!'

Nell lifted her chin. 'As my father claims he already has a buyer for the property, pray tell me what advertising you'll actually be doing? I mean, of course, if you'd prefer we took this to the authority Mr Browne mentioned earlier then by all means…'

'There's no need to be so hasty,' Byron muttered,

scrawling his signature at the bottom of the newly formed contract. He pushed it across to her.

She almost laughed when Mr Browne winked at her. 'This is now a document I'm prepared to let you sign.'

She signed it.

She turned to her father and Byron. 'The two of you can leave now. I'm busy. And I don't see any point in the two of you lingering.'

'I'll need to contact you when I have clients to show through the property,' Byron said.

'Yes, of course, but you'll do that without Roland present if you please.'

Her father's head came up. He stared at her as if he'd never seen her before.

'I'm afraid I don't trust him not to steal from me any further.' Something flickered behind his eyes and if she hadn't known better she'd have almost called it regret. 'Now, good day to you both.'

They left. She walked back to kitchen and to Mr Browne. 'Thank you for your advice. I have a feeling it was invaluable.'

'They were trying to rob you blind.'

No surprises there, but... 'You helped me gain back a little of my power. I'm very grateful.'

'It's all part of the service,' he said, gathering up his things. 'Besides, I haven't had that much fun bringing someone to their knees in a long time.'

She grinned and handed him half a dozen cup-cakes. 'Make sure to send me your bill.'

He merely winked at her again and left.

Nell sat at the kitchen table with burning eyes and rested her head against the wooden table top. She gripped her hands in her lap. She pulled in a deep breath and then another. She kept deep breathing until she was able to swallow the lump lodged in her throat. When she'd done that she forced herself to her feet. There was work to be done—another two orders to fill. And then boxes that she would need to start packing.

Mitch turned up on her doorstep on Tuesday morning, just before she was about to set off in Candy. Candy who was now running like a dream thanks to Rick.

Rick.

A burn started up in her chest, at her temples and the backs of her eyes. He'd be hundreds if not thousands of kilometres away by now. She hoped so— she dearly hoped so. She wanted him well and truly beyond her father's reach.

Oh, but how she ached to see him, hungered to hold him, yearned to know he was safe.

'You okay?' Mitch asked.

Nell shook herself. 'Yes, sorry. Please come in. Can I get you a coffee or a—'

'No, thanks, Nell, I only have a few minutes before I have to get to work.'

Right. 'I want to thank you for sending Mr Browne on Sunday. He was superb.'

'I heard. I've also spoken to him about your father's threats against Rick and he assures me that he can draw up a clause that prohibits your father from bringing any action against Rick.'

She fell into a seat and closed her eyes. 'Thank God,' she whispered. They flew open again. 'Is it watertight?'

'As watertight as these things can ever be.'

Right.

'I've also hunted up some other information that might be of interest to you.'

She gestured for him to take a seat. He did and then pulled her grandmother's ring from his pocket and laid it on the table in front of her. 'I've found out who really had this copy made.'

Her lips twisted. 'I know—my father—but he'll bribe people to lie for him and I'm not putting Rick through a trial. He's suffered enough grief due to my family.'

'It wasn't your father.'

She stared at him. 'Not…' She swallowed. 'Then who?'

Mitch glanced down at his hands and she stiffened. 'If you tell me it's Rick I won't believe you. He's not now nor has he ever been a thief. If that's what your informers have led you to believe it's because they're on my father's payroll.'

Mitch smiled then. 'You think a lot of him, don't you?'

She nodded. She loved him.

'It wasn't your father and it wasn't Rick. This fake was made almost thirty years ago.'

Her eyes felt as if they were starting out of her head. Mitch pulled several receipts from his pocket and handed them to her. She read them, blinked and then she started to laugh. 'These are signed by my grandmother.'

'During the recession in the eighties, your grandfather's business took a bit of a beating.'

'So my grandmother sold her jewels to help him out?'

'That'd be my guess.'

She stared at the receipts, she stared at the ring and then she stared at Mitch. 'This is proof.' The import of that suddenly struck her. Her shoulders went back. 'I…I don't know how to thank you.'

'No thanks necessary. It only took a little digging to find the truth. I was glad to be able to do Rick a good turn.'

She nodded.

'And it means, as far as all this goes, the ball's now in your court.'

She could now ensure Rick didn't go to jail. She could save Whittaker House. She could make her dream of a Victorian teahouse a reality. And she could make sure Rick's investment paid him back fourfold.

She straightened. She lifted her chin and pushed back her shoulders. 'I feel dangerously powerful.' And very far from *useless*.

'If you want me here when you confront your father or if you want me to haul him in on blackmail and attempted extortion charges, just say the word.'

'No, thank you, Mitch. I'd like to deal with this on my own now.'

The moment Mitch left, Nell rang Byron Withers and took her house off the market.

'But,' he blustered, 'it's only—'

'It's non-negotiable, I'm afraid, Byron.'

'Your father will be most displeased!'

She smiled. 'Yes, he will.'

Then she rang her father. 'I've just taken the house off the market,' she said without preamble. 'If you wish to discuss this any further then you're welcome to drop over at five this afternoon.'

She hung up. She switched off her phone. And then she went out in Candy to sell cupcakes and coffee.

Her father was waiting for her when she returned home that afternoon. 'You changed the locks!'

'Yes, I did.'

'I've been waiting over half an hour!'

'I told you what time I'd be here,' she returned, not in the least perturbed, unlocking the door and leading the way through the house. *Her house.* She'd become immune to her father's demands and anger. Her body swung with the freedom of it.

'Would you like coffee and cake?'

'No, I wouldn't! I want to know the meaning of this!'

'Would you like to take a seat?'

'No!'

Fine. She shrugged. 'I found out it wasn't you who had the copy made of the ring after all.'

'I told you it wasn't.'

'I didn't believe you. I also discovered it wasn't Rick Bradford who had it made either.'

The skin around Roland's eyes sagged, making him look a lot older than his fifty-seven years.

'It was Grandma herself. It seems she did it to help Granddad out of some financial difficulty at the factory.'

Roland closed his eyes, but she refused to let pity weaken her. This man had bullied and harangued her all her life, had made her feel she'd never measure up. He'd threatened the man she loved.

She lifted her chin. 'I have the receipts to prove it. So now I'm going to tell you for the last time that I am *not* selling Whittaker House. I promised Grandma I would cherish it and that's exactly what I mean to do. You can demand and yell all you like.' She shrugged—a straight from the heart *I am not useless* shrug. 'But none of that will have any effect on me.'

'I'll be ruined!'

'Maybe so, but I'm not the one who ruined you.'

He sagged, looking older and more helpless than she'd ever seen him.

'When you demanded it, I gave you my trust fund, my apartment, my sports car and I didn't even say a word when you took the majority of my designer wardrobe, but not once did you ever say thank you. You just wanted more and more. Nothing I have ever done has been good enough for you. I'm through with that. I'm not giving you anything else.'

His face turned purple. 'This house should be mine!'

'But it's not. It's mine. And I'd like you to leave now.'

He called her names, but none of them hurt. He threatened her, but it merely washed over her like so much noise. And then he left and a weight lifted from her shoulders. She would never have to deal with his demands, his threats and his ugliness again.

At nine o'clock on Thursday morning a registered package arrived; Nell had to sign for it. It was from the solicitor, Clinton Garside.

Clinton's enclosed note merely said: *Following the instructions of the late Mr John Cox.* Inside was a letter from John. Her heart picked up pace as she read it.

Dear Miss Nell,
I left instructions with my solicitor to have this sent to you if Rick should ever turn up to claim his letter. I know you won't understand my attitude to my children or why I've spoken

now after so long keeping the secret. You were about my only friend and you added the only sunshine I had in my life, so I'll try to explain it to you.

The truth is, when I was a young man, I killed someone. I was charged with manslaughter and went to jail for eight years. I've always had a temper. I was never afraid you'd be in any danger of it because you were too well supervised, but I couldn't inflict it on my children. I didn't dare. That's why I stayed away from them.

Her jaw dropped. The words blurred. Nell had to swallow hard and blink before the page came back into focus.

I could've loved the woman who had my other child, but I would've had to tell her the truth about my past and I couldn't do that.

'Oh, John,' she whispered, wiping her eyes.

So why haven't I told Rick who his sibling is outright? I stayed away in the hope it'd protect him, but he turned out too much like me anyway. He needs to prove himself and that's why I set him the test. I involved you because... Well, you were such a shy, quiet little thing but I saw the way you two connected when you were just

*little tykes. You'll know now why I chased him
away. Maybe you'll become friends after all.*

'In my dreams, John.'

*I wish you well and very happy and I hope you
don't think too badly of me.
Your friend, John.*

She folded the letter and stared at the wall opposite for a long time, wishing she could share its
contents with Rick.

Standing, she moved to the door and picked her
way through the overgrown lawn and wild garden
down to John's cottage. Rick's cottage. A path had
been worn through the undergrowth to it during the
last few weeks.

With her heart in her throat, she reached beneath
the step and her fingers curled around the key. She
rose and inserted it into the lock. She pushed open
the door and…

Her eyes filled with hot tears. Her throat burned.
Rick was gone. As she'd known he would be, but…

Some crazy thread of hope had remained alive inside her, hoping to still find him here, hoping he'd
ignored her demand that he leave.

She halted on the threshold for a few seconds before forcing herself inside the room. She immediately pressed her hands to her eyes and pulled in a
breath. If she inhaled deeply enough, concentrated

hard enough, she could still catch the faintest trace of him in the air—a scent she couldn't begin to describe, but it had his teasing dark eyes and wicked grin rising up in front of her.

A breeze wafted through the door behind her, disturbing the scent and amalgamating it with the perfume of warm grass and native frangipani instead.

No! She leapt to slam the door, but it was too late. All that registered now were smells from the garden.

She wanted to drop to the floor and pound her fists against it. She didn't. She forced herself to inspect the entire cottage—all of it neat and clean. She didn't even have the garbage to take out. Rick had done it before he'd left.

Nothing.

Not even a note.

'What on earth did you expect?' she whispered.

This was always how it was going to end—with Rick riding off into the sunset.

Without her.

With stinging eyes, she walked back through the cottage and locked the door behind her. She didn't replace the key beneath the veranda. There didn't seem to be any point.

Rick paced through Tash's currently deserted house and tried to make sense of the conflicting impulses raging through him—the urge to run and the urge to stay. The urge to jump into his car and drive until he was too tired to drive any more. Or the urge to race over to Nell's house, take her into his arms and kiss her until she swore she'd never send him away again.

His chin lifted. He started for the door.

What can a guy like you offer a girl like Nell Smythe-Whittaker?

He slid to a halt with a curse and went back to pacing.

Do something to deserve her.

Like what? He planted his hands on his hips and glared about the room. How on earth could he do that? How the hell could he prove to her that he meant to stick around? How—

For a moment everything stilled and then he slapped a hand to his forehead and planted himself in front of Tash's computer. He typed 'How to start a business' into the search engine.

And he started making notes.

It took Rick two days to register Bradford's Restorations with the business bureau, to obtain an Australian Business Number and to have business cards printed. He bought a van and organised for a sign writer. He bought tools. He hired someone to design him a website. He barely slept three hours a night.

Surely a business would convince Nell he meant to stay, would prove to her he was serious about making something of himself?

She'd believe it more if you had family ties in the area.

He swallowed and turned to the phone. Family?

Poppy? What if Poppy rejected him? He swung away to throw himself down on the sofa and drag both hands back through his hair, his lungs cramping.

What if she doesn't?

The voice that whispered through him sounded suspiciously like Nell's. He stared at the phone again. Swallowing, he pulled Marigold's business card from his wallet and dialled the number.

'Hello?'

The voice was female and he had to fight the urge to slam the phone down. 'I, uh…' He cleared his throat. 'May I speak with Marigold Somers please?'

'Yes, speaking.'

He swallowed again. 'Mrs Somers, my name is Rick Bradford and I…' How did one say it—*I'm your daughter's brother*? 'You met my friend Nell Smythe-Whittaker at the park the other day.'

'Rick!' He heard the catch in her voice. 'I'm so glad you called. I've told Poppy all about you and we're dying to meet you.'

His throat tightened at the warmth in her voice. 'I'd like that.'

'Come for dinner, please? We'd love you to.'

Her eagerness and sincerity made his heart thump. 'Promise you'll come. Tomorrow night?'

His eyes burned. He stared up at the ceiling and blinked hard. 'I…you're sure?'

'Positive.'

They made a time. He rang off and then he didn't know what to do. He knew what he wanted to do.

He wanted to go and find Nell and tell her what he'd done and have her assure him it was the right thing to do.

You haven't earned her yet.

He pulled a receipt from his pocket—a copy of the one Mitch had retrieved for Nell. It was time to see a jeweller about a ring.

CHAPTER TWELVE

NELL GLANCED THROUGH her dream folder, sipped a glass of wine and tried to find the tiniest hint of excitement.

And failed.

Closing the folder, she rubbed her fingers across her brow. Her zest for life would return. Other people recovered from broken hearts, didn't they?

She glanced at the kitchen clock. Was six o'clock on a Saturday evening too early to go to bed?

A knock sounded on the front door. She glanced towards the hallway without the tiniest flicker of interest. Maybe whoever it was would go away if she ignored it.

Another knock.

Ignoring it won't help you get over a broken heart.

She pulled a face, but all the same she forced herself to her feet to answer it.

Smile.

She pasted one on before opening the door.

The smile slid straight off again. Her heart gave

such a big kick she had to reach out and cling to the door to remain upright. 'Rick?' she whispered.

'Hey, Princess.'

Those dark eyes smiled down at her, the mouth hooked up, and all she wanted to do was throw herself into his arms.

Now there was a sure-fire way to embarrass herself.

'I... I...' She swallowed. 'I thought you'd left Sydney.' Why had he come back?

For her?

Oh, don't be deluded and pathetic. Nonetheless her pulse raced and her palms grew slick. Very carefully she released her grip on the door and wiped them down the sides of her yoga pants.

Her rattiest yoga pants. Why couldn't she be wearing one of her fifties-inspired dresses?

He shifted his weight. 'I never left. I've been staying with Tash.'

'Oh.'

Oh!

So he knew then? She swallowed and gestured him inside. 'Come on in. I was just having a glass of wine. Would you care for one?'

It took a superhuman effort, but she found her manners and managed not to sound stilted. Well done her!

'That sounds great.'

Now, if only she could pour him a glass without her hand shaking.

She didn't believe she could pull that off so she poured it with her back to him while managing a breezy, 'Take a seat.' She turned. 'Oh, and help yourself to a cupcake.' And she gestured to the tin on the table, which averted his gaze from the way her hand shook when she set his wine in front of him.

She sat. She twisted her hands in her lap. She didn't want to talk about her father. She didn't want to find out that Rick felt beholden to her in some way. 'How long are you planning to stay in Sydney?' she asked instead, determined that her stupidly optimistic heart should know the truth asap.

His grin lost its cockiness. He swallowed. It made her swallow too. 'I'm, um…planning on sticking around.'

Her fingernails dug into her palms. *He's not hanging around for you!*

'Why?' The word croaked out of her. She didn't want it to. She'd do anything to recall it, but she couldn't.

His eyes darkened. 'Damn, this is awkward.'

He could say that again.

He drew in a breath. He stood. He came around the table to where she sat and dropped to one knee in front of her. She almost fell off her chair. 'Nell, I love you and I want to spend the rest of my life with you.'

He pulled a small velvet box from his pocket and opened it. Her grandmother's diamond ring winked back at her and some instinct told her this was no copy.

'Will you do me the great honour of marrying me?'

He was offering her everything she wanted!

She closed her eyes, counted to three and opened them again. The ring still hovered there, winking at her with all of its promise. Her throat and chest burned. Her eyes stung. 'No,' she whispered. 'No, Rick, I won't marry you.'

Rick stumbled to his feet, a darkness he'd never experienced before threatening to descend around him. He stumbled around the table and back into his chair because he didn't have the strength to make it all the way to the front door.

'Tash was wrong.'

He couldn't believe his voice could emerge so normally while everything inside him crumbled.

'Tash?'

Nell's voice didn't come out normally at all, but strangled and full of tears. *Damn it all to hell!* He wished he could rewind the last five minutes and erase them. But he couldn't and he was too tired to lie. Nell might not love him, but she'd never be cruel. 'She told me you were in love with me.'

'She wasn't wrong.'

It took a moment for him to make any sense of that. When he did a shaft of light pushed the darkness back. He straightened. 'What did you just say?'

Her green eyes suddenly flashed. She leapt up and slashed both hands through the air. She paced to the sink, gripped it till her knuckles turned white and then swung back to stab a finger at him. Her hand shook and he wanted to capture it in his and never let it go.

'If you've been staying with Tash then you know what my father threatened.' Her hands slammed to her hips, the long line of her leg clearly defined in those stretchy pants, and his mouth dried. He tried to keep his mind on what she said rather than how she looked…and how much he wanted to ravish her.

'Which means you know I put Whittaker House on the market.'

'To save my skin!'

'Which means you also know,' she went on as if he hadn't spoken, 'that Mitch provided me with information to finally, once and for all, defeat my father.'

He didn't know where she was going with this— just that the pain in her eyes tore at him. He gave a wary nod.

'Damn it, Rick! I don't want a husband who marries me because he feels beholden to me.'

His jaw dropped. 'I don't feel beholden to you.' He loved her!

She gave a laugh. 'Oh, right.'

He opened his mouth.

'You've been playing white knight all your life. As a boy you tried to protect all the kids in the neighbourhood, you took the blame and went to prison for one of those friends. Heaven only knows how many women you've rescued from untenable situations since then. You specialise in damsels.'

He swallowed. Everything she said was true, but...

'I'm just the latest in a long line. Well, I don't want to be a defenceless female. I want to be strong enough to deal with my own problems.'

'You are. You have!' He didn't see her as someone who needed rescuing.

'And I don't want a white knight!' she shouted. 'When I marry I want it to be an equal partnership.'

'Damn it, Nell.' He leapt to his feet. 'Can't you see that I'm not the white knight here? You are!'

Her jaw dropped. He passed a hand across his eyes. 'You are,' he muttered, falling back into his chair.

Her mouth opened and closed but no sound came out. She stood there, staring at him as if she didn't know what to do, what to say or if to believe him.

'I've spent the last week trying to do things to earn you—to prove to you that I'm worthy of you.'

She plonked down on her chair as if the air had left her body. She reached for her glass of wine, but she didn't drink from it.

'I'm in the process of establishing my own restoration building company. I'm hoping to interview potential employees next week.'

She blinked. 'I... Congratulations.'

'Thank you.' He nodded. 'I rang Marigold and I've met Poppy. In fact I've met the whole family.'

Her glass slammed to the table. She leaned towards him. 'How did it go?'

It almost made him smile. 'Pretty well. She's great. In fact her whole family is great.' His gaze captured hers. 'She's not a damsel either.'

Nell sat back. 'No, she's not.'

Steel stiffened his backbone. 'And neither are you. You're a lot of things—maddening, stubborn, generous to a fault and optimistic in the face of all evidence to the contrary—but the one thing you're not is useless.'

Her eyes filled with tears and he ached to go to her, to pull her into his arms, but then she smiled and it was like a rainbow. 'I know.'

Something inside him unclenched.

She frowned. 'You aren't either.'

He rested his elbows on the table and dropped his head to his hands. 'Princess, I've always been able to save other people, but I've never been able to save myself.'

'Oh, Rick!'

And then she was on his lap and in his arms. He pressed his face into her neck and breathed her in. 'You saved me, Princess.' She ran a hand back through his hair and then her arms went about his shoulders and she held him so tight he could feel the broken bits of himself start to come back together.

He drew back to touch a hand to her face. 'You

believed in me so strongly that you made me believe in myself again.'

She pressed a kiss to the corner of his mouth. 'You're wonderful! You *should* believe in yourself.'

'Nobody has ever been so completely on my side before you came along.'

'There are lots of people on your side.' Her eyes flashed. 'Tash and Mitch and all your friends, and now Poppy and her family. You just won't let yourself see it. You're afraid of not being the strong one everyone else can rely on.'

Was that true?

'I went to Tash and Mitch for advice about the fake ring. Do you think that makes me weaker or less strong?'

'Hell, no! It shows how smart you are to approach the people who have the expertise you need.'

She raised an eyebrow.

His heart thumped. Slowly he nodded. 'There can be strength in reaching out and asking for the help you need.'

'Precisely.'

In that moment a spark of light lit him up from the inside, so bright it almost blinded him. He ran his hands slowly up her back and she shivered. 'Princess, you're in my lap.'

She grinned at him. 'Would you like me to get up?'

'Not a chance.'

She laughed and then gasped when he shifted

her a fraction so she could feel what she did to him. 'Oh.' Her eyes widened. She wriggled against him. 'Ooh.'

He bit back a groan. 'Steady, Princess. Not yet.'

Her face fell. 'Why not?'

He tried for mock stern but probably failed. 'There's another couple of things we need to clear up.'

She bit her lip and then nodded. 'Okay.'

'You gave me the courage to reach for my dream again.'

'It only seems fair. You're giving me the chance to chase mine.'

'I want to have a family that's the polar opposite from the one I had growing up. I want to do that with you, Nell. Not because I feel I owe you or because I think you need a man in your life to look after you, but because I love you.' A tear hovered on one of her eyelashes. He wanted to kiss it away. 'I need to know if you believe me.'

She took his face in her hands and stared into his eyes. He felt exposed in a way he never had before, but he didn't look away. 'Yes,' she said. 'I do believe you. I never thought I'd be the kind of girl who could convince you to settle down. You kept telling me how different we were and—'

He touched a finger to her lips. 'I was fighting what I felt for you.'

She nodded. 'I know that now, but when you proposed I was too afraid to believe it was for real.' She brushed his hair back from his forehead. 'But I'm not afraid any more, Rick.' And then she leaned forward and touched her lips to his and they kissed so fiercely and with all of their hearts that they were both breathing hard when they finally broke apart.

He tried to get the racing of his blood under control. 'So you'll marry me?'

'Yes.'

He slipped her grandmother's ring onto her finger. She stared at it and then covered it with her other hand and pressed it to her heart. 'How did you find it?'

'I approached the jeweller who'd sold it on behalf of your grandparents and tracked down the buyer. I made an offer to buy it back and he accepted.'

'I bet you paid twice what it was worth.'

More or less. 'I wanted to give you a ring that meant something special to you.'

She twisted around to face him more fully. 'I don't need fancy rings or fast cars or pretty clothes.'

She mightn't need them, but he meant to lavish her with all that and more.

'I don't even need this house.'

He had every intention that it remained in the family.

'I love you, Rick. All I need is you.'

'Princess, you have me for as long as you want me.'

'Forever,' she breathed.

'And beyond,' he agreed. 'Now, can I have a cup-

cake to keep up my strength before I take you upstairs to ravish you?'

She laughed and the sound of it filled him. 'I can
see we're going to have to find ourselves a good
dentist.' She reached over and lifted the lid on the
tin and offered them to him.

'On second thoughts…' He replaced the lid, lifted
her in his arms and headed upstairs instead. There'd
be time for cake later.

EPILOGUE

Mitch rushed up and clapped Rick on the shoulder. 'I have it on good authority that the show's about to start. Ready?'

'I've been ready for eight months!' Rick shot to his feet and glanced down the red carpet that led from the ornate wooden rotunda to the terrace of Whittaker House. Rows of red and white roses created an avenue for Nell to walk down. Once she appeared, that was.

Mitch took his place beside Rick, tugging at the jacket of his tux. 'I can't believe how much you guys have transformed this place.'

It'd taken a lot of hard work, but he and Nell had relished every second of it. And it had paid off. Whittaker House gleamed, apricot and cream in the warm November sunshine, the deep red accents providing a perfect contrast. His chest swelled. He'd done that. *Him!* His gaze moved to the garden—a riot of spring colour—and his pulse quickened. This was the real triumph, though, and all Nell's doing.

Nell.

He glanced at his watch and then back towards the house, his fingers drumming against his thighs. The wedding guests murmured quietly among themselves on chairs arranged beneath a red and white striped awning whose bunting danced joyfully in the breeze. A group of less than thirty people that included Poppy and her family, some of his old school friends, Nell's employees and his, as well as friends they'd made in the course of setting up their businesses—an intimate and generous-minded group. On nearby trestle tables covered in fine white linen was a wedding tea fit for a princess. In pride of place was the cupcake tower—the wedding cake—that Nell had baked and assembled herself.

It was all ready.

He touched unsteady fingers to his bow tie and then swung to Mitch. 'I thought you said it was about to—'

The band kicked up with *'Here Comes the Bride'*.

Rick turned to find Nell standing at the other end of the red carpet. His breath jammed. A fist squeezed his chest. *She was beautiful.*

She started down the avenue towards him in a magnificent 1950s frock in white silk. A scarlet sash circled her waist. Her white satin heels sported scarlet bows. In her hands she held a bouquet of marigolds. He stared and stared and his heart hammered.

She was walking down the aisle to him. *To him!*

Everything blurred. He had to blink hard. Swallow hard. 'I'm marrying a diamond of a woman,' he croaked to Mitch.

'Me too,' Mitch choked back.

Tash, Nell's bridesmaid, looked pretty in scarlet. She and Mitch had booked a date here in February for a garden wedding of their own.

Nell was setting a trend—high tea weddings.

When she finally reached him he took her hand, kissed it and held it fast. 'You look beautiful, Princess.'

'So do you,' she whispered back, her green eyes sparkling, her lips soft and her grip as tight as his.

He wanted to kiss her, but the wedding celebrant cleared her throat and he and Nell turned to her. They made the vows that would bind them together for life. They kissed—a solemn, almost chaste kiss. They signed the register. His heart grew so big he thought he might burst.

Nell leaned in against him, drenching him in the scent of sugar and spice. 'Once upon a time a girl met a boy and fell in love, but she lost the boy.'

He touched a finger to her cheek. 'Many years later the boy met the girl again and fell in love.'

Nell turned to face him, her hand resting against his chest. 'And they lived happily ever after.'

'I'm counting on it, Princess.' His throat thickened and his breath bottled in his chest. 'You've made me believe fairy tales can come true.'

'I'm going to spend the rest of my life proving it

to you,' she whispered before reaching up on tiptoe to kiss him.

Warmth washed through him. She didn't need to prove anything. His arm snaked around her waist and he pulled her closer. She'd made a believer out of him. He believed in her. Most of all he believed in them. And he made sure his kiss said as much— he and Nell, together forever.

* * * * *

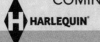

COMING NEXT MONTH FROM

HARLEQUIN

Romance

Available September 2, 2014

#4439 INTERVIEW WITH A TYCOON
Cara Colter

Journalist Stacy needs a big story—so she tracks down eligible bachelor and infamous recluse Kiernan. But soon, Stacy concerns herself with healing the heart of this controlled, commanding man....

#4440 HER BOSS BY ARRANGEMENT
Teresa Carpenter

Studio director Garret can't afford distractions—especially when they're as tempting as gorgeous event coordinator Tori. Tori knows men like Garret are bad news...but her heart has other ideas.

#4441 IN HER RIVAL'S ARMS
Alison Roberts

He may bring bad news, but when Dominic walks into Suzanna's shop she can't control her heart. Could ending up in her rival's arms be the best decision she's ever made?

#4442 FROZEN HEART, MELTING KISS
Ellie Darkins

Maya has one great passion—cooking! Her new client Will may be hard to please, but working together is shaping up to be more delicious than they ever imagined....

YOU CAN FIND MORE INFORMATION
ON UPCOMING HARLEQUIN® TITLES,
FREE EXCERPTS AND MORE AT
WWW.HARLEQUIN.COM.

LARGER-PRINT BOOKS!

GET 2 FREE LARGER-PRINT NOVELS PLUS
2 FREE GIFTS!

❖ HARLEQUIN®

Romance

From the Heart, For the Heart